Will took some g(
through, stopping to pla
the way a bit, splashing
he came back, the kid was breathing hard and chuckling, dripping all over.

He tossed over the towel, shaking his head. "You're too damned young to breathe so hard." Of course, most kids Will's age didn't run with the nasty ass scar sliding over their thigh did they? "Good looking scar. Yours is almost good as mine."

"Yeah? Cool." Toweling off those long, all the way to his damned neck legs, the kid grinned. "It was the kids that did me in. But since their mom provided the Rice Krispies and marshmallows to make the treats? Figured it was the least I could do."

"They were damned tasty, thanks." He turned over onto his stomach, his johnson trying to take interest. He chuckled at himself. You'd think one embarrassing boner in a day would be enough for any cowboy.

"Yeah? Good."

When he glanced over, it looked an awful lot like Will was staring at his ass. And Lord knew that thought wasn't helping his eager boner problem, now was it? Christ on a crutch, they were going to have to retire him to the Home for Old Cowboy Perverts.

"You, um... you okay? You kinda groaned. If you've got some sore muscles old man, I'd be happy to give you a rubdown."

Sweet Jesus.

This is a work of fiction. Names, characters, places, and incidents either are the product of the author's imagination or are used fictitiously. Any resemblance to actual events, locales, organizations, or persons, living or dead, is entirely coincidental and beyond the intent of either the author or the publisher.

Latigo

TOP SHELF
An imprint of Torquere Press Publishers
PO Box 2545
Round Rock, TX 78680

Cover illustration by S. Clements
Published with permission
ISBN: 1-933389-78-8

www.torquerepress.com

First Torquere Press Printing: October 2005
Second Printing: June 2008
Printed in the USA

If you enjoyed Latigo,
you might enjoy these Torquere Press titles:

Amnesia by Sean Michael

Bareback by Chris Owen

Cowboy Up, edited by Rob Knight

Roughstock: Blind Ride - Season One by BA Tortuga

Under This Cowboy's Hat by Cat Kane, Parhelion, and BA Tortuga

Latigo
by BA Tortuga

Torquere Press Inc.
romance for the rest of us
www.torquerepress.com

One

Dean threw the last bit of tack into the trailer, popping his neck with a sigh. Second all-around wasn't bad. Wouldn't make his retirement, but he'd make Lufkin okay, maybe even put new tires on the Dodge.

The spring air was damp, made him feel creaky, older than he ought to. Well, that tumble off Bess' Last Ride didn't help either, did it? Made him eager to get on the road, head south to bluebonnet country, though, whether it was weather or stud.

Gypsy's soft nose nudged at the trailer bars, his new girl ready to get up and get going. Dean chuckled and nodded. "Yeah, girl. We're fixin' to head out. Let me sweep this old bitch out and we'll load you up."

The pretty little paint nickered, shuffling and pushing at Blueboy's flank, trying to get the stubborn old gelding to scoot over.

"Hey." He looked over to see who else was around so early and saw a tall, skinny kid walking toward him, looking bright eyed and bushy tailed. "Don't suppose you need any help cleaning out that trailer in exchange for a ride to the next town over?"

He gave the kid a once-over, trying to place him and

failing. “That depends on which town you’re headed for. I’m headed south toward Dallas. You wanting to hit Tulsa?”

“Doesn’t matter to me. Wherever I can afford to pay the entry fees.” The kid grinned, and it lit up his whole face, changing his whole look. Well, except for the shiner around his left eye.

It was the shiner that did it. The good Lord knew he’d been loaded in the down-and-out chute once or twice. He nodded and pulled out the extra broom. “You got yourself a deal. Name’s Haverty. Dean Haverty.”

The grin got so wide that the kid winced as it stretched the bruise. “Will Benton. Nice to meet you.” Kid looked at him, head tilted. “You did all right this weekend. Just a quick once over?”

“Yeah.” He nodded, starting to clear the floor. “Can’t be too careful with their hooves. Damned vets will take your winnings in a heartbeat. You the one who pulled Devil’s Luck? I heard the cowboy on him took a header.”

“You know, that damned gelding lives up to his name. And he has a pretty hard head.” Will fell in beside him, working easily, really doing his share, which made Dean feel good about giving the kid a chance. “Smacked right between his ears and went ass over teakettle.”

“That’s a bitch. Rick Freemont did that two years ago and that nasty son of a bitch broke Rick’s hip and shoulder. Hear he’s done retired. Shame that. He was a good’un.” Sadie limped her way up the ramp, snapping at Gypsy’s tail and giving him a long-suffering look. “Hey, darlin. You ready to hit the road?”

“I assume you don’t mean me.” Will turned. “Well, hey there missy. Aren’t you a pretty lady.” Kid bent and held out a hand for Sadie to sniff.

Dean chuckled, shook his head. “This here’s Miss

Sadie. She's the mistress 'round here."

Sadie smelled the kid and then offered her dark ears to be scratched, tail wagging slow and easy.

"Yeah. You're a sweet lady, aren't you." Looked like Will liked dogs, which would make it easier to ride with him. The kid scratched ears for a few moments before getting back to work, finishing up his side of the trailer with quick, efficient motions.

Together they made short work of the cleaning and he tucked the brooms away, climbing down to unfasten Blueboy and load the stubborn beast. Gypsy'd go easy, after. Will patted Gypsy's nose and stayed out of his way, staying quiet too, which he appreciated.

He got the beast settled, murmuring low and easy, hand stroking the dark flank, before loading Gypsy up, lickety-split and locking the horse trailer. "You 'bout ready to go, Ace? I'll get Miss Sadie settled and we'll hit the road, put some miles under us."

"Sounds like a plan." Will grinned at him. "Ace, huh? Let me just get my pack, okay?"

"Yup. Sounds like a plan." He stretched up, listening to his bones crack, and then whistled up Sadie, throwing her blanket and bones in the little back seat of the truck. She needed help with the jump these days, poor old girl was feeling her age, but Doc Radley looked at her just a month ago and said she was still good to go.

He checked the hitch on the trailer one last time, gave each tire a good kick and popped the hood to check the oil.

A heavy hand fell on his shoulder, a thermos of coffee pressed into his hand. "Hey, old-timer. Heard tales you're headed to the Texas circuit. You're not really leaving us, are you, Haverty?"

Dean nodded. "'fraid so, Mac. I'm needing a bit of what ails me and I got a call from my Aunt Katie the other day. Daddy's getting to that age and if I'm a touch closer, I can help him out."

Mac nodded, red and white curls bobbing, making him look like the clown he was. "You'll be back, Haverty. You'll get to missing us and come crawling back, armadillos hanging from your mustache."

He clapped Mac's arm, laughing hard enough that Sadie barked. "The day I come crawling is the day you can put me in the greased pig competition and retire my saddle."

"Hey, there's a lot to be said for greasy pigs." Will was back, bag over his shoulder, paper bag in his hands. "Hey, Mac. Sorry I didn't know you were here or I would have gotten that pretty barrel racer to get you one, too."

Well, at least the kid knew Mac. But then, everyone knew Mac.

"I was just giving this old fart a hard time. You catching a ride with him?"

"Yeah. Need to get there somehow." That grin was back, purely infectious.

"Sadie didn't bite him, so I figure he's safe." He winked at Mac and then nodded. "Okay, sunlight's burning. Let's go, Ace. Southward ho."

"You bet. See you around, Mac." Will stowed his bag neatly in the back and hopped into the truck.

He shut the hood, the sunlight glinting off the red paint. Okay then. Back to Texas.

Ride 'em cowboy.

Somewhere in nowhere Oklahoma, Will woke up. He'd gotten in the truck, leaned against the window, and promptly fallen asleep. The radio was on low, playing classic country, and Sadie was snoring in the back, loud enough to keep... Dean, that was it, to keep Dean awake.

"Hey." Will sat up, turning the other butt cheek and stretching. "You shoulda woke me up. I could drive some."

"You were sleeping hard, figured you needed it." Dean stretched and turned down the radio. "There's Coke in the cooler behind you, you want one. We'll be in Tulsa after a bit. You know where you want to go there?"

"Nope." He tried to be as cheerful as he was clueless. No sense admitting he had no idea what he was going to do, or that if he spent money on a bus or something, he'd have no cash for his next entry fee. Dean had been nice enough to him as it was without yammering at him.

He grabbed a Coke from the cooler, stopping to pat Sadie real quick. "You want one?"

"Yeah, thanks." Dean took the can and popped the top. "I'm going to spend the night there, I think, and then head on in the morning. The Texas circuit starts up April fifteenth and I'm looking to find a campground and do some fishing for a couple weeks. Maybe Lake Buchanan or in the Piney woods."

"That sounds nice." It did, being able to take some time off between circuits. "I'll probably just try to get a job, work somewhere for a bit."

Dean nodded. "It's the cheapest way to relax I know. Campground runs six dollars a night and groceries, plus charcoal for the grill and propane for the lantern."

"Never thought of it that way." He mentally counted his cash. Maybe if he skipped the first event and did some work for some of the folks down that way, he could do that instead of having to wash dishes or do construction work.

"It's good because Gypsy and Blueboy get to ride nice and easy. There's a lake with a swimming hole, hot showers." He got a slow grin. "Big-mouth bass."

Will laughed. "My pop used to take me all the way up to Ruidoso or Elephant Butte to go fishing. He had a thing for trout. Now me? I like a nice bass. They fight like crazy." He grinned over at Dean, fighting the sudden, strong urge to invite himself along.

"Shit, yeah. But I tell you what, some butter and lemon and cook it over the fire... Sheer heaven." Dean gave him a sideways look. "You got something set up in Tulsa already, Ace? 'Cause Gypsy's needing a rider and God knows another pair of hands on the steering wheel for a piece wouldn't hurt."

"Yeah? Because Tulsa's nice and all, but I wasn't hankering to stay there." Wow. Maybe his damned luck was on the way to changing.

"It's the same six dollars a day whether there's one or ten and fishing's better with someone to jaw with." Dean nodded, then winked. "Besides, Oklahoma's no damned place to be stranded, Ace. I mean, to be so close to heaven and just miss it by one state?"

He had to laugh at that. "Yeah. Oklahoma's well.... there's a reason the south, the west and the Midwest all refuse to claim it. That's really decent of you, Dean." It was, and he meant it, and he'd do whatever he could to earn it.

"No problem. You a roper by trade?"

"Yeah. I did team roping right out of the gate, but my partner decided to go back and go to college. Then I did calf roping a bit. Now I just do the bareback competitions." He laughed ruefully, thinking it was no wonder he never made any prize money anymore. Bronc riding wasn't his strongest event.

"Bareback's a hard row to hoe. Good money in it, if you win, but the competition's rougher than hell." Dean finished his coke and shook his head, tongue swiping the drops of soda off the salt-and-pepper mustache. "Calf roping is my main thing now. The only thing I won't do anymore is the bulls. That'll kill a man, sure as shit."

Oh, yeah. He knew that one. "Damned good money there. But I'm lucky. I'm really too damned tall to ride them. Else I'd probably be fool enough to try." He laughed, sucking down his own coke.

"Yeah. I got six months in traction that tells about being all kinds of fool." The George Strait cd stopped and Alan Jackson came on. "It's fixin' to be time to eat and Sadie needs her walk. You reckon you can drive after? We could bunk down in Enid. There's a KOA there."

"Sure. Sounds good, and I was just about to need some roadside relief myself." Maybe his luck really was changing. Just maybe.

They headed down the road, stopping at a little rest stop, Dean pulling a loaf of bread and some bologna and cheese out for a quick sandwich before they headed straight on through Tulsa, the Dodge purring down the highway.

He was damned lucky he stumbled on the man and figured Dean looked like the salt of the earth type. Because bass fishing with a fine man like that was a heck of a lot better than grease and wood chips. Yeah. Definitely looking up.

They ended up at Fort Richardson, camping off the Lost Creek Reservoir.

The drive had been good, surprisingly good. Will had a great laugh and they shared a few stories here and there -- enough to know that Will came from good people, had a head on his shoulders. Dean liked the kid, trusted him enough that by the time they hit Texarkana, he could sleep in the passenger's seat.

They'd finally settled in to the campground -- pre paid for eighteen days -- threw the pop-up on the truck, got the horses settled out, and let Sadie find a shady spot to make her own. Far enough from the water that the mosquitoes wouldn't eat them, close enough that they got a breeze -- not bad, not bad at all.

"I'll unhook the trailer after a bit and run to the grocery, maybe throw a load of wash in at a laundry, grab some bait." Dean grinned over at Will who was busy being checked out by Gypsy, the curious nag nibbling and nuzzling.

"Sounds good." Will laughed, and pulled his shirt pocket out of Gypsy's mouth. "Maybe pick up some carrots?"

"I can manage that. There's a bag of 'em in the big cooler; it'll save your shirt." He opened up two lawn chairs and settled in one. "Looks like she's taking a shine to you, Ace."

"Yeah. She's a lover. Sweet and sassy. Now your Blueboy there, he's all teeth and hooves." Will rummaged in the cooler, rump up, and pulled out a couple of carrots, breaking them into pieces. "Here you go, lady."

"He's cut proud and sure of himself, that one, but shit, he can run." Gypsy whinnied, eating happily. Dean watched as Blueboy slowly sidled over, moving in on the kid. Will wasn't stupid, though, and didn't let himself get trapped, sidestepping and offering Blueboy a treat all at once.

There was a bright mind behind those pretty blue eyes, yes sir.

"Yeah? He's pretty enough, deep in the chest, nice legs." Will sat down next to him, stretching out in the lawn chair and munching a piece of carrot.

"I've had him since he was a three year old and I'd

put up with his foul temper for a hundred years to run with him, no question." Sadie wandered up and settled under his chair, groaning as she settled.

"Yeah." The kid sighed a little, watching the horses rub noses to butts. "Hey, have I thanked you for letting me tag along?"

"Only ten or twenty times, yeah." He grinned over. "And you're still welcome. So, 'fess up. What can you cook? And don't say nothin', 'cause we'll be eating nothing but chili, fish and cornbread."

"Well, I can do chili and cornbread." That laugh really was something. "But before I left home, Momma made sure I knew how to make macaroni and cheese, and steaks, scrambled eggs and pancakes, and some damned good enchiladas, those in a Dutch oven. Oh, and cobbler."

"Okay, I guess I won't drown you." He was **not** checking the kid out. Not. Not. Not. But cobbler... Oh, yeah. "Okay, you want me to pick up blackberries or peaches?"

"Whatever you have a hankering for. I like the berries better in a Dutch oven. The peaches get kinda slimy if they're not done in glass." Kid grinned at him, cheeks pinking. "I kinda like to cook."

"That's a good thing, especially if you intend to eat." He grinned back. "I've a fair hand at chili and I can grill just fine, but real cooking -- that's beyond me."

"Well let me make you a list and you can have a nice home-cooked meal tonight." Up like a jack in the box, Will was over at his pack, pulling out a pad of sticky notes and a pen, glancing over one shoulder at him. "Oh, and I can throw in cash for half."

"We'll work it out toward the end. I'm going to get some feed and a new sleeping bag while I'm out." There wasn't a damned thing wrong with his, but the kid would need one and God knew sleeping on the ground made for a sore man.

"Oh. All right." The kid scribbled, coming back and handing him a list of basics they'd need for a meal. "That should run us a few dinners and lunches besides if you get more ice for the cooler."

Not bad. Will was pretty frugal, looked like. Simple, but filling looked like the order of the day.

"You drink beer, Ace?" He'd get some bait, too, and some propane. Batteries. Coffee.

"Yeah. I'm not picky as to what kind either." Will plopped back down in his chair, grinning over at him companionably. "I'm about as easy as they come."

"Bud Lite, then." Easy. Oh. Stop it, Haverty. Now. "I got a deck of cards in the cab. Something to do once the sun goes down."

"You are one prepared man. I like that." Long, long legs stretched out in front of the kid, the patch at the knee of one jeans' leg starting to fray.

"Just used to living on the road." He slid down in his chair a bit, forcing himself to sit easy. He hadn't been so tempted to look in six years, maybe seven. Why the hell his jackass body picked now to start was beyond his comprehension.

"Yeah. I think that's my problem. I got out of the habit." Sadie nudged the kid's hand, oozing a bit so she was more between their chairs. Had to like a man your dog liked.

"I keep saying I'll settle somewhere, but I don't think it'll happen. I've been living light too many years." Will scratched Sadie's ears, loving on her with that thoughtless, natural motion that said Will was good people. "Maybe if I was still young, I'd buy me a setup and stay."

"Yeah? I can see myself staying in one place when I'm older, you know? Maybe going back to Dad's spread and taking over if my brother doesn't want it. But right now it makes me stir crazy. The whole time I was in the hospital it drove me nuts."

"Had a long stay?" Like they all hadn't, at one point or another.

"Long enough. I was in traction for a bit. Busted my leg up real good." Will unconsciously rubbed his left leg.

"Damn, that's a shame. I'm sorry to hear it." He nodded, his back twinging in sympathy.

There was that grin again. Nice to know the kid wasn't one to lapse into feeling sorry for himself. "We all do it, I guess. Dumb things, you know?"

"Oh, I wouldn't know a *thing* about doing dumb shit, Ace. I was *born* perfect." He rolled his eyes, pushed his t-shirt sleeve up so the kid could see the ridged scar where a Brahma bull had gored him. "The scars I took so you normal folk wouldn't feel bad."

"There you go." Will just laughed, loud enough that Blueboy skittered. "Most normal people would say we're both loony, Dean, doing what we do."

"Most normal people don't have the sense God gave a goat." He snorted, shook his head. "I don't know, Ace. I got a brother, a lawyer, works in a big-assed building in Houston, wears a suit and tie and does the normal thing. He don't seem a bit happier than I do."

"Maybe less. You mind if I take off my boots? They're pinching a bit these days. Don't want to stink you out, though."

"You're downwind. I'll live." They settled into a peaceful silence, watching the horses graze, Sadie snoring between them. Nice. Real nice.

The kid wiggled out of his boots, settling back again, peaceful and quiet, not wiggling around, and the next time he looked over, Will was sound asleep, head back, mouth open just a little.

He watched the kid sleep for a long time, wondering at a life that would wear a young'un out so much. Then he wondered at the fact that Will felt comfortable enough with him to rest. Eventually he stood up and unhitched the trailer, pulling the truck out slow and easy so he could do the wash and buy the kid something to cook them for supper.

As it happened, Will slept through dinner time that first day, sacked right out in the chair. Wasn't so bad, as Dean woke him up to eat store-bought fried chicken and cole slaw, which worked for him.

The second night they had fish, fried up with some bread crumbs, and the rest of the slaw. He felt lazy as Hell spending the day riding and fishing, but it was so nice, and the company was so good, that he didn't sweat it.

By the third day, Will was a lot more rested and determined to keep up his part of the bargain. So while Dean took Sadie for a nice meandering walk, he started on dinner.

Dean'd splurged a little, picking up a hunk of roast at the store, cheap enough that it would need to cook a bit, but it would work. Especially with potatoes and carrots. He got that going, searing the meat, and then adding broth and seasonings. Then he started on the cobbler.

Dean and Sadie came and went, Dean grabbing his fishing pole. By the time Dean got back, there was roast, and some of the bread he'd bought heated up, and the best blackberry cobbler Will'd turned out in an age.

"Hey. You're just in time."

"Good Lord, Ace! You've whipped up a feast!" Dean clapped him on the back, grinning from ear to ear, a couple three catfish iced in a bucket. "Oh, man. That cobbler's looking like something else. Thank you."

"Figured it was the least I could do." He grinned back. Wow, Dean looked ten years younger when he smiled like that. Not that he noticed how good the man looked all the time. Nope. Not at all.

"Let me get these bad boys covered up and wash my hands and I'll come sit." Dean whistled as he fed Sadie and put the fish away, then stripped off his old shirt and wet it to wash his face.

The man had a good build, the look of a man who'd worked his ass off his whole life, rangy and lean and tough as salt-cured leather.

Damn he looked good. And Will was staring. Crap. He looked away, sneaking peeks from under his lashes as he dished up the food. The man had pale skin where his shirt didn't cover, and just a little intriguing hair and oh, definitely crap. Maybe he should think about the worst bronc he'd ever ridden. Or being in traction.

Then Dean reached up into the back of the truck for a clean shirt, giving him a view of that strong back tapering down into a tight little backside covered in worn denim and not even traction could derail that sight.

Oh, God. He gave Dean a look, making sure the man wasn't looking, and thumped himself hard, relieved when his rising cock went down. Why the Hell he had to pick Dean, of all people to get a hard on over for the first time since his accident, he had no idea.

Dean shrugged his shirt on and grabbed a couple of beers on his way to the picnic table. "Damn, but that smells good. Where'd you learn to cook like this, Ace?"

"Told you, my momma made sure I knew how." He winked. "Doesn't hurt that I have talent for it."

Dean handed over the beer and settled, digging in with gusto, soft sounds of appreciation floating over the table.

He tucked in, too, ducking his head to hide a grin. He was tickled pink that dinner was going over so well. He slipped Sadie a bite of beef, and munched happily.

"Man, this hits the spot." Dean cut off another chunk of roast. "I saw a pretty little doe while I was fishing. Her fawn was young enough to still be wobbling. I thought Sadie was going to swallow her tongue."

"Yeah? Cool. This is a great spot, you know?" They ate companionably, exchanging the occasional comment, and Will convinced himself his quick brush with disaster was over. "You ready for cobbler, or you want to wait a bit?"

"Oh, Christ. Let's play a few hands of cards and let shit settle. I'm full as a tick."

Dean patted his flat belly like he was Santa Claus, winking.

"Yeah. I think I can see a bulge." Shit. Did he just say that? Will felt his cheeks heat. "I'll get the cards."

Dean's chuckle followed him. "It's an old timer's prerogative to get fat and lazy, young'un."

"You're not fat, lazy, or old, but I'll take your word for it, Dean." He grinned. The man was oblivious, which was a good thing. "Gin rummy? Go fish? Poker?"

"Poker'll do. There's a box of chips in there somewhere." Dean got up and started clearing, scraping the two plates and washing them in the bucket before popping them into the mesh bags to dry.

"Cool." He got everything set up, and grabbed a couple of beers, handing one to Dean when he came over. "I suck at poker, just so you're aware. Love to play it. Lose every time."

"Good to know." Dean grabbed the deck and shuffled, gnarled hands moving sure and quick. "Maybe I'll learn you a thing or two. Poker's a good skill to have."

"Yeah? Guess I've never been in a situation where I

needed it. But I'm always willing to learn." He settled in, ready to just sort of bask in Dean's easy presence.

By the time the sun was good and set, they'd put away a six pack between them, he'd actually won two hands -- out of twelve, but who was counting -- and were both laughing over one joke after another.

Dean was flushed, steel eyes bright in the light from the lantern. "Christ, kid. You gave me a stitch laughing!"

"Good. Looks like you need it." Oh, he liked that laugh, like it a lot. Too much, most like, but he'd never been called bright, had he? "Let's have that cobbler."

"Oh, yeah. Sounds good." Dean leaned back to grab two bowls and a spoon, leaving the lamplight to shine on the distinctive bulge in those jeans.

He all but banged his head on the table as his own jeans got too damned tight. Good thing he was sitting down. 'Cept he had to get up to get the cobbler. Oh, well, it was dark most everywhere but right at the table. He got up and got the dessert, slipping back into his chair without Dean noticing. He could explain it away as a stiff breeze if the man noticed, but he doubted that would happen.

Nothing was said, Dean dishing out the cobbler and giving him a healthy portion. The berries looked black and shiny in the light, the sweet juice clinging to the spoon, to their lips, to Dean's mustache.

When he found himself licking his spoon suggestively, Will told himself to get a grip. For all he knew, the man would kick his ass just for thinking what he was thinking. Maybe it had just been too long since he'd jerked off. "You all done? I'll wash up."

"Yeah. Thank you." Dean stood and handed over his bowl. "I think I need a swim, Ace. I'm going to run down to the swimming hole before it gets too chilly."

"Oh. 'Kay." He gave Dean a bright smile. Thank God.

Maybe he'd have time for a quick yank. "Have fun."

"Thanks for supper, Ace." Dean grabbed his shaving kit, a towel and a pair of little white shorts, leaving Sadie as he headed down the path.

As soon as Dean was out of sight, Will grabbed a couple of paper towels and jumped into the cab of the truck, just in case. Quick and furtive and oh, far too easily, he stroked off until he came like a house afire, picturing Dean's tight little butt in his mind. Jeez. He was gonna have to get himself under control, or this was gonna be one Hell of an uncomfortable stay. And Dean didn't deserve that, he was too nice a guy.

Dean headed out to the fishing hole at dawn, leaving Will snoring in the old blue sleeping bag. Only a week left of vacation and he was going to miss the easy life, relaxed and peaceful, good food, good company.

Real good company.

Damn.

He hadn't spent so much time one on one with someone for damned near ten years, maybe longer. Him and Timmy, they'd been an item once, lovers, partners, friends. It had been good, nice. Sort of like this.

Might have been like this forever if he hadn't been chasing the bulls still and Timmy hadn't found himself a plot of land and a man he could count on to work it.

Dean chuckled, shook his head. Gotta love old regrets. Still, it had been for the best. Timmy and... Eric, Erin, Aaron... somebody were raising calves and chickens and tomatoes and having a fine old time. He wasn't the type.

Still...

Will was enough to make a gelding hard and wanting, cut proud or not.

Shit, he was too old to be mooning. The kid was young enough to be his son. Smart though. Funny, too.

He put out a trotline and baited hooks farther down, finding himself a comfortable place to watch and relax and enjoy the sunshine and his new favorite pastime -- making friends with his left hand so that he could make it through the day without blue balls.

Hooboy.

He undid his jeans, slicking himself up nice and proper, running his palm over the head just so, pretending that the touch belonged to another pair of hands. That went nice and easy until the morning started heating a little bit and he started aching, so he wet his fingers and reached behind to fuck himself. Might as well hang for a sheep instead of a lamb.

He closed his eyes, letting his imagination wander. Thinking of a solid smile, pretty as fuck blue eyes, good hands. Oh, fuck that was nice. Not as nice as if Will was taking him, fucking him nice and hard, letting him feel it.

Christ, it had been a while.

The image was sweet as Tupelo honey and he moaned, moving his hips harder, faster, Will's name on his lips.

The crack of a stick breaking nearby sounded loud as a shot, making his eyes fly open. Not four feet away, Will stood staring at him, mouth hanging open, face red as a pickled beet.

Oh, fuck.

He went perfectly still for a heartbeat, time sort of stopping, then he was moving, yanking up his jeans, trying to figure out whether to apologize or snarl.

"Oh, God. I'm sorry. I... I woke up and you weren't there and I thought I'd come see what you wanted for breakfast and..." and the kid's eyes seemed to be glued to his crotch.

He nodded, tucking himself away, hands shaking. "Sorry. Christ. I..." He forced himself to take a deep breath and stand, shoulders tight as stone. "I should know better than that."

He walked over to the stream and washed his hands, waiting for his brain to haul itself back from where it had gone hiding.

"No. You're fine. I mean, I shouldn't have bothered you. I mean, Hell, I've been doing a lot of that since I met you." Will's eyes widened, and the red got even darker, and the kid mumbled an, "Excuse me," before turning and high tailing it back toward camp.

Dean blinked and sat down hard on the bank, watching the eddies swirl around the bobbers for a bit before he started gathering up his equipment.

Will made his way back to camp like his pants were on fire. Where the Hell had that come from? And why hadn't he left the minute he realized what Dean was doing?

Right, okay, he knew the answer to that. The sight of Dean, half naked, hands on cock and ass, well it just damned well froze him on the spot. And when he heard his name come out of Dean's mouth he almost died. The only thing that saved him was that damned stick. He'd stepped right on it as he was about to drop to his knees and start jacking off.

Will shook his head. God. Breakfast. Right. He needed to be normal and have breakfast ready when Dean got back. Eggs, leftover biscuits, maybe a fried potato. He put water on to wash dishes after, and poured himself a cup of coffee, which had finished making while he was off playing voyeur. Right. Normal.

Dean came back and dumped the gear in the back of

the truck, then walked over, cup in hand. "There enough for me?"

"You bet." Okay, it wasn't as hard as he thought it would be to be normal. This was Dean. Genuinely good people and all around decent guy. Will smiled. "Strong enough to etch steel."

"The way it's supposed to be." Dean poured himself a cup, drinking deep. "'s good."

"Yeah. I'm getting used to having no stomach lining." He sipped his own coffee, watching the potatoes sizzle. "Um, look. Sorry about bursting in on you there." He could feel his ears get hot, but damn it, apologizing was only the right thing to do.

"I'm sorry you had to see it. I..." Dean chuckled, the sound wry and amused all at once, easing the tension. "It's a hell of a position to be found in."

He had to laugh at that one, too, the humor of the situation finally catching up with him. "I bet." He cut his eyes over to Dean, glancing under his lashes, feeling mischievous all the sudden. "Looked damned nice, though."

Dean's lips opened and then he got a look, teasing and somehow hot. "How much did you see?"

"A good bit?" Shit, the memory alone was enough to make him hard. "I... I should apologize again or something, shouldn't I?"

"Probably at least once an hour for the next ten years, but we'll call it over." Dean shook his head. "Maybe I'll just tie a bell to the heel of your boot."

"Nah, just be sure to tell me you're leaving, or leave me a note or something." He shook his head, flipping the potatoes. "You want scrambled or fried?"

"Whichever you're having. I'm easy." Dean took his coffee over to the trailer and grabbed a bucket of sweet feed for the horses. "You feed Sadie this morning?"

"Yeah. I even remembered her pill." He cracked eggs for scrambling, adding a little salt and pepper, biting his tongue over the instinctive retort that came to his lips on the "easy" bit.

"Thanks." Dean pulled a cantaloupe out of the cooler and started cutting it up, peeling the wedges easily. "For the record, you're pretty damned nice looking yourself, Will. Here's the melon. I'll grab the plates."

Blinking, he looked at the cantaloupe, then at Dean's upturned rump as he rummaged for the plates. Well. Well, well, well. "Mutual admiration society," he said with a chuckle.

"Don't push your luck, Ace." The words were tough, but the tone was easy, Dean setting the picnic table. "You could be bass bait in no time."

Laughing hard, he slid the finished eggs and potatoes onto plates, along with the warmed biscuits. "Yeah, but then who would make you cobbler, old man?"

Dean chuckled. "I'd just have to settle for fried pies and remember the good old days fondly."

"Well, it's nice to know you're replaceable." He sat down to tuck in, smiling easily, the worst of the awkwardness gone. And a world of possibility opened.

The afternoon sun felt damned good, baking his muscles, legs dangling in the swimming hole, listening idly to the splashing of the two little kids farther down the way.

They'd locked camp up tight and ridden most of the afternoon in pleasant quiet, tensions eased off right quick. Then they'd put the critters out to graze and Dean'd decided to take a swim and lounge in the sun.

God, this was the life -- fishing, riding, swimming,

cobbler, blue eyes that were looking back as hard as his were. He could handle this shit.

"Hey." A towel and a water bottle thumped down beside him, along with a foil wrapped package the size of a baseball. Will grinned down at him, wearing a pair of cut offs the size of a postage stamp and some old sneakers.

"Howdy. How goes?" Dean didn't let his gaze linger -- long -- turning to ruffle Sadie's ears. "Hey Miss Sadie. D'you follow this young'un up looking to swim?"

Will grinned, those bright blue eyes taking a long gander over his own body. "Reckon she followed the Rice Krispie marshmallow things I brought for you, actually. Have at, I'm hopping in."

The kid hit the water, swimming out strong.

Well, now. He grinned over at Sadie, combing his fingers through the white ruffle on her chest. "I tell you what, lady-mine, that boy's something else, you reckon?"

Sadie stretched, groaning and settling beside him, eyes on the water.

He opened the foil packet and nibbled on the sweet, eyes watching the long body in the water, figuring that was all Sadie had to say on the subject.

Will took some good laps around and through, stopping to play with the kids down the way a bit, splashing and laughing. When he came back, the kid was breathing hard and chuckling, dripping all over.

He tossed over the towel, shaking his head. "You're too damned young to breathe so hard." Of course, most kids Will's age didn't run with the nasty ass scar sliding over their thigh did they? "Good looking scar. Yours is almost good as mine."

"Yeah? Cool." Toweling off those long, all the way to his damned neck legs, the kid grinned. "It was the kids that did me in. But since their mom provided the Rice

Krispies and marshmallows to make the treats? Figured it was the least I could do."

"They were damned tasty, thanks." He turned over onto his stomach, his johnson trying to take interest. He chuckled at himself. You'd think one embarrassing boner in a day would be enough for any cowboy.

"Yeah? Good."

When he glanced over, it looked an awful lot like Will was staring at his ass. And Lord knew that thought wasn't helping his eager boner problem, now was it? Christ on a crutch, they were going to have to retire him to the Home for Old Cowboy Perverts.

"You, um... you okay? You kinda groaned. If you've got some sore muscles old man, I'd be happy to give you a rubdown."

Sweet Jesus.

He didn't trust himself to talk, to say a fucking word, so he nodded, resting his forehead on his folded arms.

He jumped a little when warm fingers traced the scars on his back. "Oh, Hell, Dean. Mine don't even come close to this. Must have been a Hell of a ride."

"Yeah. The son of a bitch was pissed and threw me, then I got caught on the horns and he rode my ass for awhile." He'd been in the hospital for weeks, lost a good chunk of life, but with the help of God, family and friends, he'd made it. "They actually put the bull down, after. One of the boys made me a bowie knife using the horn."

"Wow. I seen a couple go that way. You were lucky as all get out. And strong." Cool lotion, suntan from the smell of it, landed on his back, and the next thing he knew his shoulders were getting a good, strong rubdown.

He moaned, breath just pushed right out of him. Oh, sweet Lord, he was never going to fucking survive this. Then again, it was one helluva way to go.

"Wow. You really are tense." There was just the tiniest hint of mischief in that sweet tenor voice. But only good, healing care in those fingers as Will worked his back and arms.

Sometimes the only way for a man to keep his sanity was to let go. He relaxed into the ground, making believe that this was perfectly reasonable, perfectly normal, not the most sensual thing he'd experienced in his entire frigging life.

Which was all good and well until Will straddled his thighs and started to really dig in deep.

The afternoon had gone quiet, the kids packed up and headed out, nothing but sun and sweat and soft moans in the air. Every so often one of them would move just right and Will's package would brush his ass and his vision would short out.

Will seemed content to just stay there all day, working him to pudding, pressing against him once and again, and the kid was hard as a rock. Finally, Will rolled off and lay beside him, stretching until he heard joints pop. "Feel better?"

He nodded, cleared his throat. "Yeah. I may never move again." Hard as he was, he might never bend in the middle again. Ever.

"You sure?" Will's hand settled in the small of his back, warm and firm. "You sound kinda rough in the pipes."

He turned his head, meeting those blue eyes. Christ, they were like a jay's wing, deep like still water and he was utterly fucked. "I'm real sure, Will. Are you?"

"Yeah. Yeah, I believe I am, Dean." Those fingers stroked his skin, up and over his scars. "More sure than I've been about anything in a long time."

There was something just right about settling things, something that eased a man's soul. Dean nodded, one hand coming out to just touch the scar on Will's thigh. The skin was warm, muscles strong; the kid was built to ride. "You 'bout ready to head back to camp?"

"Yeah. I think maybe we should." Will got up and offered him a hand, helping him up. The smile he got was like a sunbeam. "Let's go."

He smiled and whistled up Sadie as they grabbed their shit. Then he squeezed Will's hand once, real quick, before they headed back to camp.

Will led the way back to camp, acutely aware of Dean's warm presence behind him. God, he was forward, more so than he'd been in well, ever, but he just needed to get things settled, or at least started. Now that he had, it felt good, and right. Anticipation curled in his belly. It helped that he genuinely liked Dean. This was not just a warm body after too much beer.

They got there and he turned, wiping his damp palms on the butt of his jeans, grinning at Dean. "Well."

"Yeah." Dean smiled back, granite eyes twinkling. "Well."

A step was taken, then another, until they were face to face, so close he could feel Dean's heat.

He took a step, too, meeting Dean more than halfway, until their bodies brushed together. "Hi."

Dean's head tilted, eyes moving from his lips to his eyes. "Hi." One hand came to rest upon the small of his back, warm, comfortable.

Will relaxed, and the most natural thing in the world to do next was just to lean a little and put his lips against Dean's, rubbing lightly across them, feeling the tickle of that mustache against his skin. That breath brushed over his lips, one touch turning into another into another. The kisses were chaste, sweet, so quiet.

Dean pulled back a little, gave him a warm smile, then leaned up for more of the same.

There was no urgency to it, just the same comfortable silence they'd found together the last weeks. He looped an arm around Dean's neck, his other hand coming to rest on one lean hip. Dean's body came to rest against his, warm and solid. The horses milled behind them, Sadie brushing both their legs as she went to sleep under the trailer.

The only sounds were the animals, and the bugs buzzing around, and the wet slide of their mouths coming together. Well, that and the heavy, steady thump of Dean's heart. He swore he could hear as well as feel that. Dean smelled good, like smoke and water and sunscreen. All man.

The fingers at the small of his back started circling, moving slow and easy, making his skin tingle. His own fingers traced Dean's scars, fascinated with the feel of them under his hands. His mouth moved from Dean's mouth to the man's throat, finding the pulse there and pressing lightly against it. Salty and smooth and hot as Hell.

Almost as hot as the low groan that sounded, Dean's chin lifted to offer him easier access.

He wandered, tasting whatever bit of skin took his fancy, Dean's chin, Dean's ear, just below that soft earlobe where the jaw met the neck. Dean's hands were doing more than a little wandering of their own, sliding over his spine, his belly, touching his shoulders, his hips.

God, it was nice. Just exploring, getting to know what little spots would make Dean chuckle as they tickled, which ones would make him moan. The man had good hands, too, just damned good hands, gentle and warm and firm.

The sun began to set, the soft rose-gray of the sky making things seem more intimate, closer. Dean's fingers were brushing through his hair, over his nape, against his shoulder blade.

Will was feeling a little breathless, a little wobbly, and he pulled back to breathe maybe, and give Dean a smile. "Maybe we ougtha sit down if we're gonna keep doing this?"

Dean reached up and stroked his bottom lip. "Maybe we ought to feed the critters so that we don't have to stop again."

"Yeah." He nodded. They could wait. The horses couldn't. That was the way it worked. "We should."

"I'll grab the sweet feed and take care of the beasts if you'll coax Miss Sadie into her pill. She takes it easier from you."

"That's because I threaten to stop the easy flow of table scraps if she don't." Will winked, letting a deep breath calm him a bit, turning to do his share of the chores, falling into the easy rhythm they shared.

They worked quickly, the horses familiar with the routine, Sadie taking her pill after only a couple of tries. When he stood, he saw Dean putting together two sandwiches and spreading a blanket on a soft piece of ground. "This work for supper, Ace? Simple and easy?"

"Yeah. Looks good to me." He settled in next to Dean, smiling, handing over the beer he'd pulled out of the cooler.

"Thank you kindly." Dean popped the top and toed off his shoes and leaned back, munching on his sandwich.

Will stared a lot while he ate. Couldn't help it. That lean chest and flat belly just made him smile. He pushed off his own sneakers, curling his toes into the blanket, taking a long pull of his beer. This was the life. It really was.

Finally the food was done, the beers finished and set aside. Dean looked over at him and grinned. "You're a far piece away."

"I suppose I am." He grinned right back, moving close, settling his hip next to Dean's, hand coming out to sit on that flat tummy.

"Hey, Cowboy." The word was low, warm, tickling his lips before Dean's tongue swiped across his bottom lip.

"Mmmm." He moved a tiny bit closer, until they leaned on each other, hand coming up to Dean's rough cheek. "Hey."

From this distance, Dean's eyes were gray and green, with tiny flecks of blue. They were surrounded with laugh lines and dark eyelashes that hadn't started to gray yet. There was the tiniest scar over one eyebrow, shaped like an 's', a chicken pox scar right between those eyes. Those eyes were about the sexiest thing he'd ever seen, hands down. When he leaned in to kiss the second sexiest thing, Dean's mouth, their eyelashes brushed together.

Dean's hand came to rest on his waist, the weight solid, drawing him into the curve of Dean's body, finding him a place where he fit, one board into another. He liked the fit. Like a really nice dovetail joint, they just slid right together. That skin called to him again, and he started tracing patterns on it, slow and easy.

Dean's lips were soft and not all at once -- like a really fine dress shirt hung out to dry and then shook good and hard to get the stiff out. That tongue, though? That was all soft and hot, sweet against his teeth.

Will figured he was all soft by this point, because he felt like he was gonna melt. Well, all soft but one place. That was back to hard with a vengeance. There was no rush though. He could do it as slow and easy as Dean wanted, Hell, he liked it that way himself.

Titling his head the other way, Will took another kiss, finding a better angle, finding more of that beer and mustard and Dean taste. Dean stretched an arm out, giving him somewhere to rest his head. That mustache tickled his upper lip while fingers explored every inch of his spine, petting him slow and steady.

Lord above, that man could make a kiss a work of art. Long and deep and his lips tingled from the barest brush of that mustache. Will could feel the heat in his face and chest and neck.

His lips were licked and then a kiss fell on the corner of his mouth.

His jaw.

The hollow beneath his ear.

Felt so good. He chuckled, knowing Dean was following the same path he had before. He stroked the long line of that spine, just barely touching the top of that amazing butt under the edge of Dean's waistband.

"Felt so good when you did it, thought I'd return the favor." Oh, that voice was fine, rough, almost raw. Then those soft lips slid over the hollow of his throat.

"Feels good now." His head fell back, low sounds coming from his throat. Couldn't even remember the last time he's felt so good. Maybe when he got the cast off his leg. Dean nibbled the cord of muscle in his neck. Okay, maybe never.

"Yeah." Dean licked and nibbled until he was shivering, then plucked at the fabric of his shirt. "You willing?"

"Yeah. More than." Took no time at all to lean back and get rid of the cloth, coming back for more. He figured if Dean liked his mouth, he'd give it to him again, pushing his lips against that fine skin, cheek and ear and neck, all the way down to the join of Dean's shoulder.

Dean's fingers mapped his skin, learning him as sure

as anything -- arms and chest, nipples, belly, all the way down to his waistband, then back up. Moaning, Will moved into the touches, body just rolling with it. Better than lemonade on a hot summer day, this man.

They shifted, Dean ending up beneath him, their bodies sliding together slow and easy. Those eyes watched him, looked at him, still as well water. Then Dean lifted his chin and took a kiss, deeper, hotter than before.

He gave as good as he got, hands on Dean's cheeks, holding him in place for a hot slide of lips and tongues and bodies.

A hand cupped his ass, holding him, lining their cocks up so they could move together. Dean's moan slid down his spine like old leather -- heavy, slick, smooth as shit and undisguisable.

Oh, damn, that felt good. Been a long time since he'd been anywhere near this close to a man, and Dean wasn't just some random fella. He was, well, Dean, and he was hot and right and Will stroked that hot chest under him, fingers finding one tiny nipple.

That hand tightened, Dean's knees parting and bending, cradling him. Dean's nipple wrinkled, grew tight and hard for him and the kiss grew hot, spurred on between them. He was hot and hard, too, hips pushing down against Dean's, zipper of his cut offs pressing hard against his trapped cock. It was as good as it was agonizing.

"Will..." Dean's lips left his with a gasp. "'m too old to shoot off in my jeans. We need to figure whether we're stopping here or traveling on."

"Don't want to stop, Dean. But there's no hurry for anything, you know?" He chuckled, feeling his prick throb. "What I mean is, we don't have to go too far too fast, but I sure would like to get in your pants."

His hand was taken and pressed against a thick bulge,

then up to the button of Dean's fly. "There's no shrinking violets here, I'm thinking."

"Certainly doesn't seem to be shrinking." Laughter was so easy with this man, but it was time to be serious a minute. He looked right into those clear eyes and nodded. "Want you."

"Yeah. I'm wanting you, too." His face was stroked, and then Dean gave him a slow, warm smile. "I'll show you mine, you show me yours?"

"You bet, old man." He basked in that smile a moment, then pulled back to sit on his knees, opening his cut offs with a sigh of relief.

A strangled noise sounded, one callused finger sliding down the length of his shaft.

"Oh, God." Yeah. Just like that. His own hands went right for Dean's fly. "You did promise to show me yours."

"Yeah. I just... Some things a man needs to touch." Dean scooted closer, fingers wrapping around him.

His fingers stuttered, and he swallowed hard, hips moving sharp. "Oh, Lord. Dean."

"Yeah. Lord is right. You're fucking fine, Ace. Fit nice." Dean leaned in, licked his shoulder, breathing hard.

"Oh." He scrambled, pulling at Dean's stubborn zipper, wanting hot skin of his own to touch. When it finally opened and Dean filled his hand, all he could do was moan.

"Shit, Marthy," Dean panted, shivering under his hand. "You'll drive a man mad."

"What a ride, though." Will squeezed. Nice and thick and so hot it liked to burn him. Reluctantly, he let go just a second, wiggling out of his cut offs all together before stripping off Dean's jeans. Then he settled back on top of Dean, rubbing their cocks together.

"That's the ticket. Lord, yes." Solid as a yearling calf under him and steady as a racehorse, Dean didn't waste a bit of time, hard and hot as all get out.

"Yes." It was, damn it. Just what he needed. He kissed Dean again, hard and needy now, sliding against the pretty cock, feeling them getting each other all wet.

Dean gasped, back arching up in a bow beneath him, hands cupping his ass and holding tight. That mouth opened for him, wide and needy, hungry.

They wouldn't be long, he figured. They were just off like a house afire. Slow to start, flash to the finish line. But if it felt as good to Dean as it did him, that was all that mattered. He pushed Dean's legs open wide and pressed down between them, getting some good friction going.

Dean's lips slid to his ear. "Close, Will. Got me hotter than a two dollar pistol. Last longer next time, swear it."

"S'okay. S'all right." He just couldn't make words beyond that. Could just push and push and finally yell his head off. So long. It had been so long. Felt so damned good.

Dean came quiet, only a soft grunt against his neck and that body was shuddering to beat the band, liquid heat spreading between them.

They rested together, breathing hard, bodies going slack and heavy. "Oh, damn, old man."

"Tell me about it, Ace." One of Dean's hands slid slow and easy, petting. "That was something else."

"Sure was." He dropped a light kiss on Dean's lips. "Thank you."

Will got a quick grin. "Well, I'm thinking we got a decision to make, Ace."

"Yeah?" Thinking. Sure. He could do that.

"Mm-hmm." Dean nodded. "We're gonna have to figure whether we're gonna get all weird and pissy or whether we want to do it over and over again. You got any thoughts on that?"

"Well, I'm not much for second guessing, Dean. So as long as you don't get all het up on me? I'm thinking we'll do this over and over. Sound like a plan?" He wasn't holding his breath. Really.

"I'm thinking it would take a damned fool not to take hold of a good thing, Will." He was given a chaste, quiet kiss, a pat on the ass. "Ain't nobody ever called this old boy a fool."

"Good. S'that settled? 'Cause I think a nap is in order." Nuzzling Dean's neck, he smiled, happy in his bones.

"Yup." Dean's arms wrapped around his waist, body settling.

They'd work out all the details later. For now it was enough to know that all that chemistry between them was no lie, and that they had all the time in the world to explore it.

Two

Not bad. Will rubbed his bruised hip. Not bad at all. He'd taken second for the night, fourth overall for the weekend on the bareback broncs. Not enough to get anything but his fees back, but that meant he could get into the next event.

Now it was time to catch up to Dean, who was loading the trailer, and who had done a Hell of a lot better than he had, coming up with an all around second. Nice. Maybe they could have steak or something.

He got there just in time to load Blueboy, talking the skittish old fart into the trailer with little trouble.

"Hey, old man. Still got room for me?"

"Always, Ace." He got a warm grin and a welcoming nod. "You were looking good on the broncs. You settle out okay?"

"Well enough to go on. You did all right, for an elderly gent." He winked, scratching Sadie's ears as she leaned on his legs.

"Oh, ho! Watch it, young'un or you'll be hauling that ass over hill and under dale." Dean fished out a pair of longnecks, tossing him one and leaning against the truck. "I been having a bit of a think, actually."

"Yeah? I thought I smelled smoke." Oh, he liked

laughing with this man. He popped the top, waiting for Dean to go on.

"Nah, that was your ass skidding on the ring." Dean chuckled. Nodded. "I'm thinking I'm using Blueboy for the next handful of shows and Miss Gypsy's sitting fallow. No reason she can't earn her feed for you."

He looked at Dean long and hard before he nodded. "Sure. That's mighty good of you, Dean. I appreciate it."

Dean nodded, finishing his beer. "Don't mention it. You got plans?"

They'd managed to go their separate ways for a few days, Will staying with a friend of his folks because he always did when he came this way and it seemed rude not to. He'd had enough of old man Hayler, though, and was hoping Dean wouldn't mind his company again.

"Nope. Just figured I'd maybe have some supper, learn some more poker tricks?" He tried hard to keep his voice light, not expectant.

"Sounds like a plan. Only thing is..." Dean gave him a quiet look, a serious look. "I got me a room for the night. Proper shower, swimming pool and everything."

"Oh." He wasn't sure if he was invited or not. "You mind if I come over for a bit? Since it's got all the nice arrangements?"

"I was sorta counting on more than a bit, Ace." Dean pinked a hair, just a touch. "Got a king-sized bed."

"Yeah? That's a lot of space." Will grinned, moving closer, just a hair. "Think they have a hot tub?"

"I reckon." His grin was answered, those granite eyes twinkling. "We could grab some fried chicken on the way over, spend the good money on a proper breakfast?"

Shit, that sounded better than good. "I think that could work out real well."

He was handed the keys as Dean grabbed a second

beer. "It's the Comfort Inn off 35. You're young and agile, you're driving."

He laughed. "You bet." They got in the truck and got settled, and he allowed himself the luxury of a small touch, hand resting on Dean's thigh for a tiny moment.

Dean caressed his fingers, hiding the touch in the action of turning on the stereo. Randy Travis. Not bad at all.

The ignition turned over and he was suddenly more than ready for that hotel room. "Maybe we should grab a shower and a nap and then get us some dinner. We can still grab fried chicken at the grocery."

"I could more than live with that. There's a Waffle House nearby, worst comes to worst." Dean shifted, hand moving those tight jeans about.

Eyes on the road, Will, he thought. Just keep it between the lines. "Now that would be a fine breakfast. Steak and eggs and hash browns scattered and smothered."

"Hell, yes. Nice pot of coffee, some moo juice, buttered toast." Dean nodded. "After. There's a full-sized shower waiting."

"Oh." He kept it to the speed limit, despite the urge to speed. Last damned thing they needed was a ticket. He pulled in just about the time he thought he'd go crazy peeking at Dean, and backed them in horizontal across from their room.

"You wanna walk Sadie or check the horses one last time?"

Despite the bruises, he knew he wasn't as stiff as Dean, had seen the careful way the other man moved. "I'll walk Sadie. You check the nags." He truly had to like a man who put the animals first. "Be back in a bit."

He clipped the leash on Sadie, who grumbled at him, but in a busy parking lot it was best.

By the time Sadie'd done her business, Dean had

locked the horses up tight and pulled their gear to the tailgate, along with the dog bowls. "We're right there."

Then he was given a view of a fine cowboy backside, moving sure and steady toward the door. He'd follow that tiny butt just about anywhere. They unloaded their stuff and made sure Sadie was fed and damned if there wasn't a king sized bed and a full size shower.

"Shower first?" He smiled, feeling like he could finally move close. Maybe sneak a kiss.

"God, yes." That familiar grey Stetson flew over to the chair by the lamp. "I've been thinking on that for days, Will."

"Yeah? Me, I've just been thinking in general terms. Like maybe this." He took Dean's face between his hands and pressed their lips together, just light and smooth.

Oh, yeah. The flavor of hops and mint from those damned toothpicks and Dean slid over his tongue as those lips parted eagerly. Dean encouraged the kiss to deepen, solid body hot against him.

He slid his hands into Dean's back pockets, cupping that amazing butt in his hands. The kiss was just what he needed. Dean's arms wrapped around his neck, callused fingers rubbing his nape.

"Mmm." Felt good. Bronc riding made a man's neck stiff. Dean made other things stiff. "Whatd'ya say we move this into the bathroom? Get a little closer to that shower."

"I can get behind that." Dean took a step, then another, slowly dancing them back toward the bathroom, ass rubbing into his hands the whole way.

Oh, that was something he'd have to do with this man someday. Dancing. He'd bet Dean was a devastating dancer. Right now he just wanted the naked kind though, and he squeezed his double handful, nibbling Dean's neck.

Dean's hand slid around and started working on his shirt, hot tongue sliding over the edge of his ear. "Shit, Will. Your mouth."

"Mmm. Yeah." He helped out as much as he could with the clothes, but he wasn't really willing to let go. "You feel good."

"Want you." Long fingers worked open his Wranglers, slid them down so those rough fingers could stroke his prick. "Mm... yeah."

"Oh, Hell." He danced back a little, finally letting go to reach for the front instead, opening Dean's jeans and finding hot flesh.

Dean bit down on his shoulder a bit, enough to feel it, enough to feel good. "Skin, Will. Water. Been wanting."

"Yeah. Been missing you a good bit for such a short time, Dean." He grinned, pulling back by mutual assent, both of them stripping down in a hurry. Dean started the water and he stepped in with the man and closed the door before they touched again, else the shower might not have happened.

There were some sights to be seen in this world -- sun over the mountains, newborn colt finding her feet, a perfect ride -- then there was Dean Haverty hard as nails with water pouring over that sun-cured skin. Damn.

Hot as Hell and twice as naughty, the thoughts that went through his head. He'd settle for acting out about a third of them. To start. He put his hands on Dean's ribcage, one hand sliding down to cup a hip, the other moving up to Dean's chest, thumb scraping one tiny nipple. The skin tightened right up for him and Dean moaned, reaching for him. They moved together, bodies hot and wet, slick together, Dean's tongue fire on his collarbone.

"Damn, old man. If I'd known what you could do in a shower I would have shelled out for a hotel a week ago." He chuckled, hand on Dean's hip drawn back to that finer than fine ass, tracing the curve of each cheek.

"I'm just full of surprises, Ace." Those lips parted, fastening onto the big vein in his throat, sucking in time with his heartbeat. Oh. Hell, yeah.

Head falling back, he held on tight as his world just spun. He rubbed, water pouring over them, slick and good and right. His cock was pumped, palm sliding over it, running over the tip and setting him afire. "Fucking fine, Will. So fucking fine."

All he could do was moan and return the favor, taking Dean's prick in his hand and pulling lightly, rubbing them together, feeling the incredible heat they made together.

Dean's face lifted, moans harsh, needy as that hot mouth found his ear. "I want you, Will. Want you to take me. Tonight."

"Oh, God." He wanted that, so bad. "Yeah. Shit, yeah."

"Oh..." That sound was sheer need, Dean's hips pushing faster into his hand. "Sweet Jesus, I want you."

The idea, the feel of Dean against him, that rough hand around his cock, it did him in, and Will groaned long and loud, coming hard. The last of his groan was swallowed up in a hard kiss, Dean's mustache soft on his lips as those lean hips pushed that cock against his palm over and over.

He squeezed, thumb rubbing, figuring if he held on tight he wouldn't fall down. When Dean came, the moan was soft, low, almost lost under the water.

Almost.

They leaned on each other, whooping for breath until the water ran cold. "Shit! That's my ass that's freezin." Will chuckled, hauling his chilled butt and Dean out of the shower.

Dean was laughing to beat the band, tossing a towel over at him, and giving him a nice long gander of cowboy body all dripping and loose from coming.

"Damn, you're a sight. And once we get some food in us and that bed under us I figure on getting a close up." Will grinned, toweling off.

"As close as you reckon you can manage, cowboy." Dean had lost ten years of hard work and rough living in that shower. Will was going to have to make sure the man had them more often.

He'd have to make damn sure. He couldn't wait to see what a king sized bed did for him.

Oh, Dean was **pissed**. Someone had gotten into the stalls and fed half the horses bad feed. Now they were all fucking colicky, all sick and fuck if the vet didn't cost money on top of not being able to ride.

He stormed into the hotel room, slamming the keys on the table. They ever caught the motherfucker who did this? He'd force feed them soured milk and duct tape their fucking mouths shut and watch 'em drown.

Hurting critters.

Cowardly asshole.

Will sat straight up on the bed, hair sticking up all over, eyes blinking wildly. "Dean? What's going on?"

"Goddamn motherfucking bastards went into the friggin' stables and fed the critters spoiled fucking sweet feed. Not going to kill any of 'em, but they're fucking sick -- damn near half the fucking stable!" He was pacing, shaking he was so pissed. "Damnit! Some of those show ponies are getting on in age! Hell, my Blueboy's no three-year-old!"

"Oh, fuck!" Will scrambled up and out of the covers, bare ass flashing him. "The colic? They need anyone to walk them? I can come help." The kid reached for the clothes tossed over a nearby chair.

"Whoa, Will. We're all taking turns. Rodeo people brought a shitload of volunteers out. Miss Lacey's in fucking tears and apologizing." Dean shook his head. "We're not due back out 'til after noon, though I reckon we'll go sooner."

Hell, he'd have stayed longer, but the more cowboys that came out, the more pissed off everyone got and he was already tied in a knot.

"Oh. Okay." Will yawned wide enough for him to count teeth and sat on the bed, jeans held loosely in both hands. "What d'ya wanna bet it was one of those yahoos that think rodeo is cruelty to animals?"

"I don't know, but I fucking find 'em, they're gonna learn a thing or three about cruelty and animals."

A sharp nod showed Will's agreement. "You know it. You okay?"

"Yeah. No." Dean shrugged, put his hat on the table. "I'm pissed as hell. I hate this shit."

"C'mere. Lose the shirt."

He arched an eyebrow. "I'm not sure I'm fit company to sit too close, Ace."

The bright grin he knew so well appeared. "You will be when I'm done with you. You keep saying I got good hands."

He started unbuttoning, that smile sparking one inside him. "That you do, Ace. That you do."

He got up and walked to the bed, toeing off his filthy boots first.

"There you go." Will watched him, reaching into the bag at the end of the bed for some baby oil they'd picked up at the truck stop a few towns back. "Let me pummel some of that pissed off out of you."

"Don't make me laugh now, Ace. I'm having a true-blue snit." He took off the belt and pulled out his wallet.

"Am I losing the jeans?"

"Well, they do have a distinct odor. 'Sides, they'll just get oily." A wink joined the grin.

"Smartass." He gave Will another grin, an honest one this time and shimmied out of jeans and socks, leaving him in his fruit of the looms.

He made his way to the bed and sat with a tired sigh. "I'm all yours."

"Yeah. And you're worn to a frazzle from the looks of you." Warm concern lit those blue eyes, and Will eased him down on his belly, moving to kneel at his feet. Warm hands, slick with oil, started a firm massage at his arches, digging into his sore feet.

"Oh... Oh, sweet Jesus and Mary, that's good." He moaned, long and low, and damned if the massage didn't warrant it, too.

"Yeah? Good. I can see why you're so wound up, but it can't be good for you." A tiny string of kisses landed on the scars on his back before Will moved on to his calves, turning them to jelly.

Oh, Lord. He was never going to move again, just melt right here on this ugly as hell motel bedspread.

Humming lightly, Will worked up to his thighs, really pushing and pulling there, getting right at the tense muscles. Kid was pressed against him now, knees between his spread legs, warm and good.

"Shouldn't be legal to feel so damned good." His voice wasn't sounding even a little pissed now, just a little husky, a lot rumbly.

Will chuckled, just as husky and darned happy. "Glad you approve, cowboy." Those hands skimmed his ass, patting lightly. "I'm saving the best for last."

Dean felt his cheeks heat and he chuckled. Ace did have a thing for his ass. He wiggled, just a little, just enough to catch attention.

"Mmm. Nope. Shoulders next, Dean." And damned if the kid didn't straddle his ass and start working his neck and shoulders. Just making the sore and mean melt right out of him.

"Ohh... I'll give you until forever to stop that. Damn..." Will was healing stiff places he didn't even know he had.

"You got it." More oil drizzled down his spine, Will working the big muscles on either side, rolling his shoulder blades, making it all go away. "'Sides, you feel good."

"I feel like a million bucks." He damned near whimpered when Will started finding those tight little knots that rode him so hard.

"Got that right, Dean." Will wiggled against his ass, hard shaft suddenly making itself known. But the massage never stopped, just worked him until he swore he was more liquid than solid.

Oh, shit, this was good. Not just the massage -- the care, the company, the touching. Will.

When Will finally got to his ass he was flopping around like a rag doll, and the kid dug in, just pressing deep, and who the heck knew that would feel so good? The massage ended with a kiss pressed to the small of his back and Will stretching out alongside him, one arm across his waist. "Better?"

"Uh-huh." He scooted a little closer, blinking slow. "Lemme give you a thank you kiss?"

"You bet." Will leaned in, their noses bumping.

"Mmm..." He took a long, slow kiss, still too melty and relaxed to push it, just enjoying Will's mouth.

Letting him set the pace, Will petted him, hand warm and still oil slick on his back, keeping him loose. Oh, he was spoiled, sure enough, spoilt rotten and damn, didn't he love it. He caught Will's tongue, sucked it gently, mouth making promises he intended to keep. A soft moan carried through on Will's lips, sinking into him. Still treated him like a sore colt, though, careful touches, just keeping it on low burn.

"Want you, Will. Want you in me, nice and slow and easy." Best way to get what you needed was to say. God knew he wanted-- wanted something slow and sweet. Something good to dream on.

"I can do that, cowboy." Will nuzzled his neck, right where it met his shoulder. "You want to face me, or you want to spoon?"

"Whatever melts your butter, Will." He grinned, rubbed his cheek against Will's. "I'm easy."

"Oh, yeah. One of the things I like about you." Slow but sure, Will turned him so they faced each other, pulling his top leg over one slim hip.

"Everybody needs a talent, Ace." He stretched easy, hips tilting to make things easier.

"You've got a ton of those, Dean." Those sweet lips nibbled his, teasing his upper lip, his cheek and ear. Oily fingers found his ass, sliding between his cheeks, pushing lightly against him.

"Mmm..." He shifted a little, taking the fingertips in and letting them slip out, moaning against Will's shoulder.

"Mmm. Now you're all nice and relaxed. That's damned nice." One finger slid right in, deep into him.

"Oh... " He bit into his bottom lip, head falling back as he rode, undulating like he was neck-deep in pond water.

Will gave him just what he needed, scraping his throat with sharp teeth, finger moving in him, one shifting out, two pushing in.

"Sweet Lord..." He arched, moving a little faster, body rippling. Oh, that set a slow burn inside him, all green wood and smoky.

"So hot. Gonna burn me right up, Dean." Will slid

those long fingers out and tilted his hips just so, pulling his leg up even higher. That long cock nudged his balls. "Shit."

He reached down, shifted until he could guide Will to his entrance, rocking in tiny motions against the flared head.

"Dean. Damn. We're don't have rubbers." Will rested against his forehead, breath coming in sharp pants.

He took a deep breath, forced himself to back off, ease away. He wrapped his hand around Will's cock, pumping easy. He was the one who'd started this do-si-do, he'd not leave Will wanting.

A short, sharp sound met his touch, Will pushing into his hand. Then Will reached for him, too, hand closing around him. "Oh. Oh, damn."

Dean took Will's lips in a long, hard kiss, cursing the universe at large for shit like colicky horses and nasty fucking diseases and being a forgetful jackass and he was going buy a friggin case of them this afternoon. He rubbed his thumb over the head of Will's cock, pushing all that bullshit away, looking for their pleasure.

The kiss came back to him, hard and strong, Will looking just like he was, hand pulling at him. They started moving faster, harder, tugging firm, pushing at the slit with every upstroke.

"Dean!" Will thrust hard, thrashing, moaning loud and long as spunk spilled over his fist. That callused hand never stopped moving on him, the kisses never let up.

Didn't take him long to find his own pleasure, tongue sliding into Will's mouth as he shook and gave it up with a low sigh.

They settled together, breath slowing along with their hearts, and for awhile it all did go away, warm and lazy as time slowed like molasses in winter. Dean just closed his eyes, tired down deep in his bones.

"Get some sleep, cowboy. I'll wake you when it's our turn to go out and help." Will stroked his back, a slow, even touch that lulled him.

He nodded, resting one hand against Will's soft, smooth inner thigh. Yeah, that would work. That would work just fine.

Dean pulled out his good summer shirt, checked his best jeans, dusted off his dancing boots. Then he called to check times at Charlie's Steakhouse, pulled out some good CDs and put them by the stereo.

God, there was no fool like an old fool and damned if he didn't fit the bill.

Still, there was something to be said for dating and taking care and if Will didn't like it? Dean reckoned the good old boy would just say so.

He went ahead and put some lube near the headboard, some condoms. He was thinking maybe they ought to talk about that -- he was hankering to learn Will's flavor and they seemed pretty one-on-one. Still, Will was young and young men liked sowing oats.

It was damn near dark before he was all settled and waiting on Ace, watching Troy Dungan go on about the weather, little bow tie bobbing.

The knock on the door came just when he figured he was going to nod off, the weather forecast long since over. But it was unmistakable, just like Will calling out, "Hey, cowboy. You in there?"

"I am. Hold up a sec." He got the door open, taking himself a bit of a look before stepping back. "Come on in."

"Hey, cowboy." Will grinned at him, turning his hat 'round and 'round in his hands. "Sorry I'm late. Your

Blue? He was hard to settle tonight."

"Yeah? He okay?" He frowned a little, not quite fretting.

"I think so, yeah. He wasn't looking wild around the eyes, or sounding colicky anymore. He was just stampy." Will looked him over, good and hard. "You look like dinner."

"I was thinking steak, maybe, and then dancing here..."

"Oh." Those blue eyes just twinkled at him. "And you say you're old. I'd better shower quick, then. I smell like the wrong end of a steer."

"Oh, you just smell like you been working. You need me to press a shirt for you?"

"Would you? You're not my mom, I know, but they're all gone to wrinkle." Will laughed, walking over to kiss him, careful to keep away from his clean shirt. "I'll be out in a few."

"It's hell living out of a case, Ace." He dug out Will's shirts, grinning to himself as he knew right where Will kept them, pulling out two and the can of starch and making short work of them.

"It is." Will's voice echoed out from the bathroom, and soon enough the water was on, then off. Will took short showers by himself, like a child of the desert usually did. Made Dean smile to think how much longer those showers were when he was in them.

Of course, there was something about all that skin, wet and slickery and soapy and fine under his hands...

That fine body he was thinking about came out with Will's head attached, wearing only a towel, hair dark with water. "Oh, you did the blue stripe. Bless you."

He nodded. "It looks fine on you."

He wandered over, leaning in to lick the water drops off Will's shoulder.

"Mmmmm. Tell you what, Dean. You'd better watch it or there will be no steak. And I'd hate for you to be all dressed up for nothing. You look fine. Really fine."

"Oh, Charlie's is the best steak in town and Thursday's cheesecake night." He went all pink, belly clenching. Damn, Will had a sweet tongue.

"Cheesecake. I'm in." He got another kiss, short but sweet enough to put color in his face for a whole 'nother reason, and Will moved away, stripping off the towel to put on shorts and jeans. "So, did you hear about Tally Jessup? They say he's got a concussion, but he'll do all right."

"Yeah? Good deal. He's a good'un. They decide to put that bull down?" The sonofabitch hurt every cowboy it'd come across in the last season.

"I think so, yeah. He's not just a good athlete, you know? He's a killer." That shirt he'd pressed looked awfully nice buttoned up and smoothed on. Will sat and picked up his boots, cleaning the worst of the dust off before pulling them on. "So," Will said, standing and turning a circle for him. "Do I pass muster?"

He licked his lips, mustache tickling his tongue. "Yessir."

"Good." Grinning some more, looking happy as a pig in shit, Will wandered over, putting a hand on his waist and leaning in, lips brushing his. "Let's take each other out and show off a little."

"I'm right behind you." He tossed Will the keys to the truck and opened the door to the fine summer night, the lightning bugs flickering and buzzing.

Oh, that was fine. Damned fine.

They chatted amiably on the way, which was part of the good about Will. They could just talk, or not, and it didn't matter which. Laughing about the new kid helping out the clowns this season and his bruised ass took them all the way into Charlie's and through ordering, and darned if Will wasn't flirting with him shamelessly, just like this was their first time out and Will really did want to show him off.

By the time the steaks came out, they had each had a beer, then they both switched onto tea. The meat was quality, the potatoes big as Dallas and the company? Well, shit, that was just what a man needed.

Leaning back and patting his belly, Will echoed his thoughts aloud. "That was damned fine. Maybe we ought to get that cheesecake to go, wear off some of this by dancing first."

"Oh, now there's a plan." He nodded, finished his tea. "I'm thinking that cheesecake'll be fine in a few hours."

In bed.

"Me, too." Oh, that got him a slow grin and a wink. And a nudge under the table from Will's boot.

The desserts came and he got the check and then they were up and ambling, bellies full, both of them all happy smiles. Will drove them back to the motel, singing along with the radio, teasing him about his old folks station, just having a ball. Couldn't beat a night out like that. Unless the night in went even better.

He pulled his hat off as soon as they got in, heading over to pop the disc in the stereo, George Strait filling the air.

"Mmm. Good choice." Will caught him up on the way back, the cheesecake set on the table and Will's hat on the chair. "Wanna dance, cowboy?"

He opened his arms, nodded. "Yes. Please."

Will moved into his arms so easy, so right, like he just belonged there, and started moving him around the room, one hand in his, the other settling at his waist. Sooner or later they'd trade off, because Will couldn't lead worth a damn.

Still, the feel of their bellies and hips brushing together, the feel of Will's breath on his cheek as they sang along? Made up for any awkward bits and moving around the big bed.

They ended up sorta wedged along one side of the bed, swaying side to side, Will's hands in Dean's back pockets as they moved. Felt good, felt real good, and the most natural thing in the world was for Dean to tilt back and Will to bend and for them to kiss, nice and slow.

His hands wrapped around Will's shoulders, lips parted and offering Will all he had. Give and take, that's what it was, because Will gave back, one hand moving up his back to stroke his spine, his neck, lips opening under his, tongue coaxing his into Will's mouth. The sound that left him was rough and raw, leaving no doubt how Will was affecting him. He pressed into that soft heat, tongue moving, licking. Will met him head on, tongue playing his, hands moving again to untuck his shirt, so they were suddenly skin on skin, Will's hands on his back.

"Oh..." Finer than frog hair and twice as precious, those hands. His own fingers started working buttons, baring that flat belly.

"Mmmhmm." Wiggling, Will helped him, getting the nice, neatly pressed shirt off and both of them let it fall to the floor, not caring one little bit. Will kissed him some more, fingers counting each scar on his back, each bump of his spine.

Will's skin was hot, just soft to his fingers and he let himself trail a path along the waistband of those tight jeans.

"Oh. Yeah, Dean." That grin was bright as day, even though it was good and night now, and Will sucked in that belly, gave him room to move. Even before he touched the top button he could tell Will was hard. Wanting.

"Oh, that's..." His fingers slid in, stroking the wet tip

and he met Will's eyes. "I'm wanting to know how you taste, Will."

Will looked at him, long and hard, searching. "You mean without? I'm willing. Hasn't been anyone but you in... awhile."

"I mean without. I haven't since Timmy and we were safe." He backed off a little, giving Will room to choose.

"Well, as long as you're sure you wouldn't rather have cheesecake." The joke was a good try, but it fell a little flat, Will looking so damned young all of a sudden, uncertain, but with something that looked a lot like joy coming to those eyes. "Yeah. I haven't ever not used a rubber, Dean."

His heart lurched and he stepped forward, bringing them together again, bringing them close. "I've been thinking on it, Will. Thinking about how you'd taste to me."

"Yeah? I don't think I let myself think on how you'd feel." Those rough hands were on his cheeks, Will's lips closing over his. "Want to, though."

"Yeah." Dean whimpered, whimpered like a starving man offered a banquet. "Bed?"

"Naked. Bed." They both moved, hands working on what was left of their clothes before stumbling the rest of the way to the bed and falling on it. "You just take my breath, cowboy."

"Yeah, you're something else." He brushed their lips together, then slid down, finding one hard little nipple.

That got him a moan, Will wiggling, getting so Dean had more room to move, looking down at him with wide eyes. Working his way down each rib, Dean didn't linger, didn't tease, just headed for the taste he was needing.

Will stretched out on his back, long legs spreading for him, cock flushed dark red and hard, the scent rich and right. He took a deep breath, drawing Will's musk into him before sliding his tongue over the tip, pressing. Tasting.

Sweet Lord in Heaven.

"Oh. Dean. Oh, God." Will's voice was rough, harsh, the breath just rasping right out of Will's chest. That cock actually twitched for him, if anything got harder for him, and he could see Will's thighs and belly ripple.

"Will..." He moaned, taking the hot flesh in, sucking and pulling, asking for more of that flavor.

He got it, Will arching into him, pushing into his mouth. Will's hands moved from his head to his shoulders and down his arms, like Will wasn't sure where to put them, and the kid was moaning steadily, gasping and grunting.

God, yes. He moved faster, taking Will all the way in, swallowing hard. His fingers were sliding along those long thighs, massaging.

"Please. Dean. I. Oh, you feel so good. Hot." And Will tasted good. Salt and earth, all male.

He hummed, nose brushing the mass of curls the color of sweet hay. Yeah. Yeah, Will. So good.

Those strong thighs rose as Will dug his heels in, Will's hips pumping up, thrusting into him. "I'm gonna. Dean. Yeah."

Yeah. Will was close. Dean could feel it in the way Will's balls drew up tight, see it in the deep flush of Will's skin. He rolled Will's balls, careful, encouraging Will to give it up, let him taste.

"Dean!" That was it. All it took, and Will shot for him, giving him what he wanted, hot and liquid and so, so good.

Dean took it all, pulling, moaning, hips rocking against the bedspread.

Will was just shaking under him, panting, hands patting his shoulders. "Oh, Lord."

He took his time, cleaning Will's cock before lifting his head, meeting those wide eyes. "Damn. That was... damn."

"That sums it up pretty well." Those eyes had the most stunned expression, wondering, hot. "C'mere."

Nodding, Dean worked his way up 'til their bodies were just right together. That was just what he'd needed. Just perfect. He couldn't wait until they could do it again.

Three

The fish were biting, the afternoon lazy and warm, the company damned fine.

Dean gave Will a long, slow once over from where the man was leaning against a tree. Yep. Damned fine.

Dean slapped at a horsefly, stunning the big-assed thing and tossing it out in the water.

Will glanced up and caught him looking, grinning wryly. "They must like your rubber worms better than my real ones, Dean. I'm not getting a thing."

"Yeah? You're in the shade, bet they're biting deeper. Water's cooler there." God, how many times had he heard his daddy say that? "Still, bad fishing's better than working."

"Hell, yeah." He got just the tiniest hint of mischief in the look sent his way. "'Course, so is making out like teenagers."

"The way you talk!" Dean grinned. "I thought making out like teenagers required an old Chevy and a moonlit road out where the state troopers wouldn't see you."

"You say tomato, I say tomahto." Stretching, Will reeled in his line, setting his pole aside. "Well, then how about we just skip the teenager thing and go right to the

'I'm wanting you, cowboy?'"

Oh. Oh, yeah. He could handle that shit. Dean started reeling in, body going hard as a rock in his Levis. "I never could understand the teenage-appeal."

"Well, I admit, I didn't either, but that could be because I wasted those years trying to like girls." Will was chuckling now, moving right up to him and grabbing him.

"I thought you were a slow learner, Ace." He moved right into that long body, hands sliding over that flat belly.

"Sometimes you just have to pound things into me." Oh, the boy was in a mood today. Hot, callused hands slid up over his back and neck, massaging.

"Mmm..." He leaned into the touches, shivering to beat the band. "I don't know, Will. I reckon you ought to consider pounding something into this old boy."

"Yeah? I'm thinking that's an awful good idea, Dean." Will nibbled at his lips, rubbing against him. "Just let me get something from the truck?"

"Yeah. Yeah, I can handle that, Ace. Just..." He leaned up and took a hard, hungry kiss, taking a taste.

"Yeah." Breathless, eyes dark, Will gave him one last press of lips before scampering off, long legs pumping.

He watched those legs until he couldn't see them, then went about the business of pulling in lines and popping his catch into the basket in the water. Damn. Damn, he had it bad.

It only took Will a few minutes to get back, jeans pocket bulging as much as the zipper of those jeans bulged. The kid came right back up to him, body running right up against his, lips meeting his in a kiss.

He let himself cup that hot bulge, tongue pressing into Will's lips with a low moan as his thumb traced a line down that shaft.

"Mmm." Will moaned against his lips, hands falling to cup his ass and squeeze. Kid really did have a thing for his ass.

Sorta worked out, given that he was offering it over. Just the thought made his cock leap, made his fingers tighten up. "Will."

"Yeah. Where the heck did we put that blanket after lunch?"

"Behind the cooler." His lips followed Will's jaw, breathing in the sweat and salt and musk there.

"Mmmhmm. 'Kay." Will tilted so he could reach the sensitive spots, pushing into the touch of his hand, legs spread wide for balance. "Think we can get to it?"

"Mmm... get to what? Fuck, you taste good."

"So do you. Jesus." Will moved, slow but sure, swaying, kissing him, but moving back toward the trees. Lo and behold there was that blanket, and Will spread it out with the toe of one boot, pulling him down as Will sank to his knees.

He went easy, cock too hard for a cat to scratch. Working Will's t-shirt up out of the waistband, he kept on tasting that salty skin. Moving into his hands easy and natural, Will grabbed his shirt and did the same, pulling it out of the way so they both touched flesh, sweet and hot. They worked themselves back on the blanket, side-by-side, his hands drawn to Will's back, Will's skin.

Will was a little more focused, tracing his skin right down to the waist of his jeans and popping the button. "Want to see you, Dean."

"Yeah." He leaned a bit to undress, lips wrapping around Will's nipple and sucking hard. Two birds, one stone. Hooboy.

"God." Will got his jeans down, hands finding his bare ass and stroking, squeezing, just playing to beat the band.

He got Will's fly undone, then moved away with a moan, hand going to his own heel. "Boots. Fucking boots."

"Here. Let me." Will yanked and tugged, hauling his boots off, then starting on his own beat-up ropers. While Will was at it he shucked out of his own jeans and shorts and Lord that boy had legs.

Dean lost his jeans and knelt up, hands sliding along those fine legs, lips tracing the line of curls crowning that long cock.

"Oh. Damn. Dean." Will seemed to forget what he was doing, hands stuttering on his shoulders and back before sinking into his hair.

"Shit, yes." He shook, tugging gently at those curls, fingers tracing the soft inner thighs. Lean muscles flexed and gave under his fingers, and the smell of hot man filled his head. Little noises and filthy words fell from Will's lips, the kid a Hell of a lot louder like this than he was any other time.

Dean whimpered, leaning up to taste that tip of that cock, sucking it deep as the first flavor hit his tongue like an explosion.

Yes. Oh Christ, yes.

"Oh, good God, Dean. Your mouth!" A single thrust pushed Will's cock in hard, sliding into his throat, every muscle in that long body going tight.

He wrapped his fist around the base of Will's cock, squeezing tight. "You spend now, Will, you swear you'll get it up again for me. You've been promising me a hard ride."

A soft wail sounded, and Will went very still, eyes closed, breathing deep. "Got no doubt in my mind I could, Dean. You'd raise a dead man. But I want in you now, not an hour from now."

"Yes. I've been needing." He scooted back, careful

not to touch too much, eyes sliding hot over that body. "How do you fancy me?"

"Any way I can get you." Those blue eyes opened, burning right through him. "But that depends on you, Dean. On how it will be best for you." The kid grabbed his discarded jeans, fishing out a tiny tube and a little foil packet.

"It's been going on seven years since it's been more 'n my own fingers on a regular basis, Will." He met those prettier-than-fuck blue eyes and smiled. "I reckon you'll take care of me, one way or the other."

"Yeah." The smile he got was downright blinding. "I want to see you then. On your back." Will crawled over and kissed him. He leaned back against the soft blanket, mouth opening wide, kiss growing deep, needy. Will gave him deep and needy, tongue pushing in, as that fine body settled between his legs and rubbed against him.

Oh, fuck. Oh. Dean's knees lifted, ass rubbing up against that heat. Oh, he'd been waiting so frigging long.

The kiss finally broke, Will biting gently on his lower lip before kneeling up and getting the lube open, slicking up two fingers and pressing them against his hole. "You ready for me, cowboy?"

"I think I was born ready for you." He shifted toward the touch, looking to feel Will deep.

The look he got liked to burn him alive. "Then I'm coming in." Those two fingers slid right in, stretching him, making him feel it, but so slick and gentle there was no pain. None at all.

Dean moaned, heat moving up from his toes, flushing through his whole body like an August grass fire.

Will's free hand moved in circles on his belly, soothing him as those fingers pushed in, then out, opening him. Kid was focused, tongue just sticking out enough to see the pink tip, hips rolling just the tiniest bit as he pushed

Dean higher and higher.

Was the sexiest thing he'd ever fucking seen.

Still, he'd been riding his own fingers for seven years and there wasn't a damn thing on him that was going to be breaking from this ride. He reached down, one of his own fingers sliding in along with Will's, making them both moan.

"Jesus, Dean! Thought you wanted me to be in you when I come. You keep that up it'll be a near thing." Will pulled away, leaving him feeling damned empty, but the kid was pulling on a condom and getting all greased up for him, so who could complain? Before long Will reached over and grabbed his wrist, easing his hand away as well, settling back between his legs, cock nudging him.

"God, yes." His toes curled and he waited, letting Will have the reins. "Want to feel you deep."

Nodding, Will flexed those strong hips, pushing into him, filling him, going deep. A short pull back, and a deeper thrust pushed Will in. The kid didn't stop until he was all the way in, hips fitting against his ass, hot skin pressed to his.

His eyes met Will's, throat working as he tried to say something, anything about how sweet it was, how hot. Not a fucking word came out though, just a sweet, long moan. Will just nodded again, eyes knowing, and started pushing, in and out, muscles rippling, panting for breath.

They found their rhythm, bodies moving like their heartbeats, steady and growing faster and harder. Will's hands slid under his ass, lifting his hips, spreading him wider before bending and taking a kiss, deep and hard. He ground down into Will's hands, onto Will's cock, crying out his need into Will's lips.

Nothing that hot could last long, and soon enough Will lost the rhythm, hips snapping out of time, hands leaving bruises on his skin as the kid worked toward a big finish, words pouring out of that sweet mouth again, landing on his lips.

He found his cock, tugging hard, pulling so his hand touched Will's skin, feeling them both.

"God. Fuck! Dean." Will gave it up for him, hips slamming him as the kid cried out, head falling back as he came.

"Shit, yes." He leaned up, tongue sliding over Will's throat, shooting hard enough to rattle his back teeth.

"Oh, damn." They tumbled to the ground, breathing hard, Will petting him randomly, deep happy noises coming from Will's throat.

"Yeah." He let his hand rest on Will's belly, fingers moving slow. "Damn."

"That ass of yours is gonna kill me some day." The prospect didn't seem all that distressing, if the smile on Will's face was any indication.

"If them legs on you don't kill me first." He goosed one inner thigh, grinning. "Fine cowboy."

Will grinned. "Yep, you are that." They were quiet for a bit, and he figured Will had dozed off just about the time the kid leaned up on one elbow. "So, you think the fish are biting now?"

"Could be. 'Course you'll be assured a better catch with that mouth than you ever would with those dead-ass worms." Dean winked. "I caught us enough earlier to manage supper."

"Well, then. We'll just have to pass the time some other way." Will snuggled up to his side, head coming to rest on his shoulder. "You good, old man?"

"Fine as frog hair, Ace." He nodded, kissing that soft hair.

Yep. Damned fine.

He was getting old

It was fixing to rain. He could feel it in his hands, in his back, in his knee. Nothing like waking up with a hitch in your getalong.

Dean groaned, pushing himself up off the ground. They had a tent in the truck and he'd best put it up now before the storm than struggle with it later.

Damned rain.

Damned storms.

Damned old bones.

Damned... his eyes caught a glimpse of blonde hair peeking out of the blue sleeping bag. Well, okay. Will he liked.

One blue eye cracked open and peered at him over the edge of the bag. "Whatcha doin'?"

"Tent. Rain." He cleared his throat, running his hand through his hair. "Then coffee."

"Mgnuhn." He took that as an affirmative on the coffee, and Will crawled out of the sleeping bag and went off to do his business, coming back to help him set the tent up. "Some nasty clouds."

"Mmmhmm. Rains hard enough, won't be riding Friday." He pulled the sleeping bags inside, making them a nest.

"Might be nice to have a break. That old bitch I had Saturday really pulled my left shoulder." White teeth flashed at him in a bright grin. "Oh, now. That looks cozy."

The sky answered for him, a sharp clap of thunder making Sadie bark. "Yep. Let's put the tarp up so we can cook dry and we'll slide back in."

"That sounds like a plan." They worked quick and easy together, setting up the tarp, and Sadie immediately moved under it. She'd be safe and dry there.

Will grinned and pointed to the tent. "After you."

He chuckled, bending over to climb in, giving Will a nice long look at his ass.

A small moan was his reward, and Will followed him in, bowling him over for a kiss.

"Mmm..." He wrapped his arms around Will's shoulders, lips opening.

The kiss was nice and slow and thorough, Will exploring him like they'd never kissed before. Kid did love to taste him. They found a comfortable place, side-by-side in the sleeping bags. One kiss melted into another and another, his hands sliding over Will's back, Will's belly.

Will rubbed at his back like the kid knew he was hurting, massaging as they kissed, relaxing him as well as arousing. The rain started up outside, a gentle patter on the tent walls, giving a sweet rhythm to their touches.

He moaned, feeling easy and warm, lazy and horny all at once. "'s good, Ace."

"Yeah. It's fine. Really fine, Dean." Warm breath fanned his cheek as Will worked toward his neck, licking and nuzzling.

"Oh..." His toes curled and he reached around to cup Will's ass. Talk about snuggly and horny in the morning.

"Mmm." The big tendon in his neck got a nibble, the hollow of his throat a long taste, and Will grabbed his butt as well, squeezing.

"Oh, damn you have a fine ass, Dean."

He rocked back into Will's hands. "You want it, it's yours."

"Now that's what I like to hear." Will rewarded him with another kiss, deep and searching.

Oh, yeah. He pushed toward Will, rubbing against his lover as the kisses made him dizzy as being bucked off a temperamental bull.

"Want you." Warm and callused, Will's hands slid

under his shorts, pushing them down his legs and stroking his hip, his butt.

"You got me." He returned the favor, baring that prick and ass to his hands.

"God. Yeah." A single finger stroked along his crease, Will bending to take one of nipples in that hot, hot mouth. The rain came down harder, pounding against the tent, making it almost steamy inside.

Loving this man was like that one ride, the one you tell about at the bar, the one that stopped the entire fucking world from moving. Dean moaned, one hand sliding into Will's hand just to hold on.

Will licked and nibbled and sucked hard on a patch of skin that no one would see but him, finger circling his hole over and over. He spread, riding that finger sure and sweet, needing that deep touch.

"Just let me..." Will moved away for a second that seemed longer than an eternity, but when the kid came back his finger was slick, riding in deep, pressing him open.

"Yes." He arched up, so much better than his own hand. So hot. "Will. 's good."

"So hot for me. So tight." The words fell on his skin, hot and damp and full of need. The one finger became three, pushing him so far open he thought he'd split in two.

A groan was pushed out of him, low and deep, rocking him inside and out, his cock a brand where it slapped against his belly.

"Want in you, Dean." Hard and hot against his hip, Will rubbed, teeth grazing his nipple again, making it throb.

"Yes. Now." His belly jerked, muscles going hard in response to sheer need.

"Yes." Quick as anything Will had a rubber on, and

was pushing him into place, spreading him wide and settling between his thighs. "Hell, yes. God, you taste good."

"And you feel right." He pulled his legs up, slow and careful, giving Will a nice, long look at the ass the kid kept reaching for.

A rough, low sound spilled out, sounding like it was torn from Will's chest. Then the head of that sweet cock was against his hole, pushing in, Will's face set in hard, needy lines.

Dean forced his eyes open as long as he could, watched every damned second, every look in those clear-water blue eyes until the pleasure was just more than one cowboy could ignore.

In, a deep, slow slide and Will was in all the way, balls swinging against him. "Fuck."

Will bent to kiss him, taking his mouth hard, making his head spin. He wrapped his legs around Will's body, arms holding tight as his world was upended.

Sweat dripped on his chest and belly as the tent steamed up, Will pushing into him over and over. Slick skin rubbed against his, sharp teeth caught his lower lip, and it was one Hell of a ride.

The thunder started shaking the road, the lights and sounds just making it better, sharper, making him clench harder around Will as they worked.

"Yeah. Oh, God, yeah, Dean." That boy was damned fine above him, hair curling up, skin flushed deep, muscles standing out hard, and Will matched the sound of the rain, pounding him.

He reached down, started tugging his cock in time, toes curling, soft, pleading cries fighting the thunder for attention. He had to compete with the noises Will made, too, hard needy sounds that tugged at his cock as much as his own hand. Will looked down at him, pumping hard.

"C'mon, cowboy. Wanna feel... gotta. Come for me."

Oh, shit. The things that came out of that fine mouth. Dean came with a cry, grinding down hard on Will's cock, fucking flying.

Eyes wide and hazy, Will went still while he squeezed and worked that cock, then Will's hips snapped, pushing hard against him as Will came, whole body shaking like he was out in the storm instead of safe and dry in the tent.

Dean had just enough sense to catch Will when he came forward, holding the lean body close.

Will mumbled something that sounded like, "flying" against his neck, settling in, damp and warm.

"Mmm." He nodded, stroking slow and easy. "Good."

"Mnh." Will chuckled. "You melted me, cowboy."

"Good to know. Reckon I'll make it a habit." He kissed Will's temple. Best cure for the morning grumps he'd ever found.

"I'll count on it, then." They snuggled, listening to the rain outside, and damned if his old bones didn't feel one hundred percent better.

God, it was hot.

Now, Will knew from hot. He did. When you grew up in Deming, New Mexico, hot was a way of life. But this weather wasn't just hot. It was stifling. Even the flies didn't have the energy to buzz.

Swimming wasn't cutting it. The damned water was just as hot as the air. The cold washcloth on the back of his neck worked for all of ten seconds. He was grumpy as Hell and twice as hot.

"Hey, Dean? We got any ice?"

Grey eyes glanced over at him, Dean just sitting perfectly still in the shade of the truck. "Cooler."

Right. That meant moving, but heck, it couldn't be worse than the way he was now. Maybe he'd create a breeze.

Will rolled to his feet and headed for the cooler, opening it and closing it as quick as he could to keep out the heat. Ice. Oh yeah. A whole great big handful. Will wrapped it in his washcloth and rubbed it against his neck. Oh, yeah.

"Damn. That's the ticket."

"We ought to run up to Wal-Mart and buy one of them kiddie pools and about ten bags of ice." Dean was watching him close -- not moving, mind you, but watching.

"Oooh. That's a damned good idea." He grinned over at Dean, picking out a piece of ice and tossing it at the man.

Dean caught it, started sliding it over the dark throat, over the bare chest, water trickling down to pool in Dean's bellybutton.

Shit. That made him hotter than the weather. "Maybe we should do that tomorrow. I think we've got enough ice for today." He took out another piece and let it slid over his own skin, water running from his throat down over his breastbone.

"Ace, it's this hot tomorrow? We're getting a friggin' room with an a/c." The water in Dean's bellybutton spilled over, darkening the waistband of Dean's trunks.

His mouth was suddenly dry as trail dust. "Yeah? I like the sound of that, too. Crank it up right on the bed so we have to snuggle to get warm."

"Hell, yes. Keep the blinds closed and keep us skin-to-skin all day to keep from freezing." Dean's legs shifted, spreading a little bit, giving him a glimpse of those inner thighs.

Will knew his own trunks had to be showing what a good idea he thought that was. Damned if it wasn't possible to get hotter than he was before. Another piece of ice flipped from his hand to Dean's, and he got to watch the water run down to stop at one of Dean's nipples, causing it to draw up. "Yeah. You, me, a lot of strenuous exercise."

"Mmmhmm." Dean's eyelids were heavy, tongue pink as he licked his lips. "Can't be worrying about frost-bite, can we?"

"Nope. I mean, how would you explain that in July? In Texas?" God. Will put a cold hand down his front to adjust himself, but it didn't make him go down even a teeny bit. Dean was just too tasty.

"We'd have to do some damned quick talking. Best off avoiding the issue altogether." Dean shifted and the bare tip of his cock peeked from the edge of those little shorts.

"There you go." Oh, he wanted to touch that, but well, that would make them hotter. Then Will hit on a good idea. He wandered over next to Dean and sucked a bitty bit of ice into his mouth before plopping down and leaning over to lick that bit of skin.

"Jesus!" Dean jerked, legs parting, eyes going wide. "Will!"

"Mmm?" Well, he figured that would either cool Dean off or melt him all together, and either one would be better than sitting and sweltering.

He worked his way under the shorts, chilled fingers pulling them down and away, reaching for Dean's balls.

"Cold. Christ. Will!" Dean's voice was just as coarse as sandpaper, heat pouring up off the lanky body.

Well, the skin there sure was drawing up, but the cock in his mouth was pure fire, growing with each suck, so Will didn't worry too much on it. He just kept doing what he was doing, until his lips met the base of Dean's prick, using his tongue underneath.

Dean's hands ghosted over his head, his shoulders, hips shifting, moving, pushing up toward him.

So good. Sweat was just dripping off him but Will couldn't remember where he'd set the ice down, didn't really care. Nothing was better for what ailed him than Dean. He grabbed Dean's hips to hold the man steady, and rose up to lick around the tip of that sweet cock, gathering up the stronger taste there.

"Oh, Christ, Will. You make me need." Dean writhed like a man afire, which was damned close to the truth now, wasn't it?

They were gonna go right up in smoke. "Yeah. Always want you." He did, too. He went back to his happy work, licking and sucking like Dean was a popsicle.

One of Dean's hands started working open the drawstring on his shorts, searching for his cock with blistering fingers.

Oh, God. Yeah. Will moved, turning just so, letting Dean have access to him. Felt like nothing else in the world, Dean's hand around him. His own hand slipped beneath Dean's balls, searching for the tight heat inside the man.

"Yes..." Dean gave him a sweet little whimper, then started working him like a master, that palm dancing over his hot flesh.

Yeah. Hot and right and good. So good. Will humped Dean's hand and sucked Dean's prick and slid a finger deep, pushing in, and forgot all about the damned Texas weather.

Dean rode his finger, took his mouth, all the while whispering impossibly hot little promises that sounded so damned good, so fine.

Made his head spin, made it hard to breathe. The scent of them together was wild and hot, and his skin slid against Dean without any need for lube. There. His finger found the spot he was looking for, and Will scraped over Dean's gland, knowing he couldn't last much longer.

Dean gasped, cock jerking, bouncing on his tongue before shooting, fingers tightening around his shaft, tugging hard.

Will moaned, licking at Dean's wet heat, hips jerking as he came all over. Damn, that Dean made him hotter than a two dollar pistol.

"Shit... you are something else, Ace. I mean it."

"Mmm." Will grinned and nuzzled Dean's belly. "Well, I figured if we were gonna sweat, we should at least have a reason. We got any of that ice left?"

"Shit I hope so." Dean grinned and winked. "We gotta get cooled off enough to find ourselves a nice hotel room, don't we?"

"Oh, yeah. With air conditioning." Then they'd find another way to beat the heat. Will grinned, giving Dean a slow kiss. Not that this way was bad.

What a rotten damned weekend. Both he and Dean had taken a drubbing, he in the bronc riding, Dean in the calf roping. Will was tired and aching and he'd snapped at Dean like a rabid dog earlier.

They'd both withdrawn into silence, handling their regular chores with the horses and Sadie without a word, heading back to the hotel with some fried chicken to lick their wounds. Dean wasn't giving him the cold shoulder or anything, or pouting, thank God that wasn't the man's way. Will knew Dean just respected his foul mood, and was giving him time to crawl out of it.

And damned if it wasn't time to kick his own ass out of the doldrums and apologize. Will took the rest of their stinky chicken wrappers and bones out to the dumpster, then came back in and washed his hands, toeing off his boots and going to sit on the bed across from where Dean sat in the little club chair.

"Hey, cowboy. Sorry about that earlier."

Dean nodded, looked over with a half-grin. "Been a shit day in the all-around, yeah?"

Will blew out a breath, and nodded, his own grin answering. "You know it. Feel like I've been tied to the tail of a dust devil all day long." Will winked, patting the bed next to him. "Let me make it up to you?"

"Let's settle on just meeting in the middle and I'm there." Dean moved over, one hand sliding over his belly. "Hey, stranger."

Oh, yeah. He could get behind that idea one hundred percent. Will did some touching of his own, hands resting on Dean's shoulders and rubbing. "Hey. Been a Hell of a few weeks, now I think on it. Think I'm needing some of this." The kiss started out slow and careful, but didn't stay that way long.

Dean's hands -- rough and callused, but still so good on his skin -- cupped his jaw, tilting him so that the kiss could go deep. He was tasted and touched, that cowboy could kiss, could spend a lifetime just making him dizzy with one touch of lips after another. So good. Took the rest of the world away, those kisses. Made him forget there was anything but time, and the slide of Dean's tongue in his mouth, wet and hot and tasting like beer and chicken and those little peppers Dean ate like candy.

They settled back together, pressed together lips to knees, Dean's hands exploring his thigh, his hand on Dean's spine.

The bumps and ridges of Dean's back, the sweet curve

of that fine ass, the ticklish spot at the base of Dean's neck, all of them got a thorough exploration. And as soon as he got that shirt off the man, he was gonna do it again.

One of Dean's legs slid between his, pressing, rubbing just a little, denim on denim scratching under the sounds of their moans.

The press and rub of the seam in his jeans against his cock jolted him, made him moan and break the kiss. "Clothes off, Dean."

Dean gave him a throaty little chuckle. "I'll show you mine, you show me yours."

"You got it. You first." Will grinned and attacked the buttons of Dean's shirt.

Dean wasn't any help, working at his belt, his fly, kissing and nibbling and distracting the fuck out of him.

The distraction proved too much for him when Dean pulled his cock out of his jeans and wrapped that workingman's hand around it. Will let his head fall back, eyes closing at the feel of it. "Dean. Good."

"Yeah... So hot, Will." Dean's mouth fastened on his skin, licking the line above his opened collar.

"Damn. You make me hot." He wasn't sure he was making sense, and he didn't care. Will opened his own shirt, and helped Dean pull his jeans off. "Your turn, Dean. Want that skin."

"Yeah." Between the two of them, they managed to get naked, both hissing as their skin met.

The smooth skin of Dean's hips filled his hands as he worked his way toward that butt he was so fond of. He nibbled at Dean's throat, mood improving by leaps and bounds with every touch.

Dean's hand was still wrapped around his prick, thumb sliding and rubbing and it liked to kill him, the slow waves of pleasure.

Little shockwaves of pleasure kept shooting up his

spine and popping in his head, and he just couldn't get a handle on what he was supposed to be doing. So he let Dean do the doing and floated, touching and rubbing and pushing into that sweet touch on his cock.

Dean took another long kiss, fingers moving a little faster, grip a little tighter.

"Dean." The kiss broke and Will moaned, riding it, balls drawing right up with it.

"Mmmhmm. That's it. Come on." The words were soft, drawled out against his jaw, wicked sweet.

Oh, Hell. Took less than no time for that tight, hot grip to make him lose it, the sound of Dean's voice, rough and low, making him shudder and shake as he came right into Dean's hand.

Dean's groan was trailed along his skin. "So good."

"Mmm. Damn. Yeah." He was out of breath, like he'd been thrown right off a bucking nag and piled in the dirt, but this was a lot less painful and a lot more fun. He let go of his death grip on Dean's ass. "What do you want, cowboy?"

"Hmm?" Dean was still nuzzling and licking, rubbing against him slow and lazy.

A low chuckle escaped him. Damn, that Dean was easy to please. And Will purely loved to please him. He pushed a little, rolling Dean to his back, going in for another kiss. Dean went easy, legs cradling him, hips rubbing up toward him.

Hands on Dean's shoulders, Will kissed the man until they were both breathing hard again, and damned if he wasn't getting hard all over, too. A quick shift of his weight let him at Dean's chest, and he pinched one tiny nipple, licking at the stubble on Dean's chin.

"Oh, hell." Dean shifted, moaning low, hips sliding on the sheets.

Yeah. That was what he wanted. Those little hitches

in Dean's breath, the little needy movements. He went looking for more, lips wrapping around the nipple he'd just left, fingers going to play with the other.

He heard Dean's fingers fisting in the sheets, felt as that sweet cock grew wet-tipped.

He'd get there. First he needed a taste of that flat tummy, warm and firm, moving with Dean's breath, muscles shifting under skin. The taste there had more salt, and hints of his own come, and Will licked and nipped happily.

"Oh, Will... Damn. 's good. Real good." Dean was twisting, almost humming with want.

God, he could smell what he was doing to the man when he bit down on one hipbone, and when Dean's cock nudged his chin it was hot enough to brand him, and wet. He needed some of that so bad, so he just opened up and took Dean in, sucking and licking.

That brought Dean's shoulders up off the mattress, those granite-chip eyes staring down at him in passion-drunk amazement. "Will! Oh, Christ."

"Mmm." Will hummed, letting Dean know how good it was, how right, and worked his way down as far as he could before coming back up to lick at the spot just under the head. One hand stroked Dean's belly, elbow bent to hold him up, the other went straight for the soft skin of Dean's balls.

Dean started gasping, sinking back into the sheets. "Please, Oh, so good. More."

Well, he aimed to please. So he gave more, sucking to beat the band, tongue moving up and down, rolling those sweet sacs gently before pressing against the skin behind them.

"Close. So close." Dean jerked, panting, shudders rocking his lover.

Oh, good. So good. Pure man, hot and saltbitter and

Will wanted it all, wanted to drink Dean right down. He pulled hard with his lips, one finger sliding into Dean's hole, just a bit, humming deep in his throat.

Dean spent with a long, low, almost-pained cry, entire body moving as his mouth was filled.

Savoring every drop, Will licked the head of Dean's cock as he pulled off, his own prick still hard but not urgent. So damned good with Dean. Always so good. The man looked dazed, and Will smiled at Dean as he crawled up to take a kiss.

Dean was warm, melting, lips soft and open for him, eyes dazed and sated. "Damn, you make up pretty, Will."

"You inspire me, cowboy." Sure enough, he wasn't joking. Dean was worth making up with every time. Especially when Will was the one at fault. He settled against Dean, cock in the hollow of the man's hip, legs tangling together. "You're purely worth it."

"Mmm..." One hand settled on the small of his back, petting. "Next time we'll just pretend to have been rumbly, yeah?"

"Sounds like an idea." He did some petting of his own, soft touches with no intent or direction. Will chuckled. "Like this a lot better than I would you cleaning my clock. Glad you're so darned reasonable, Dean."

"Life's too short to live pissed off." He got a grin and a kiss. "Beside, we got life kicking our asses for us, no reason to help."

"Yeah." Good philosophy. And now that he had his grumps fucked out of him, Will could maybe live by it, too. Life was good.

Watermelon. Beer. Peach ice cream. Burgers.

Sweet as fuck little camping ground outside of Sun City.

Dean toed off his boots, popped a top, and leaned back in his chair, letting the sun soak off the last touch of soreness from Killeen. This was the life, yessir.

"A man could get used to this, Dean." Will plopped down at his feet, ignoring the other chair, and stretched out, balancing a beer on that flat belly.

"Mmmhmm. Not gonna get me complaining, that's for damned sure." He smiled down, admiring the long line of Will's body. "Not even a bit."

"Me neither." Will grinned up at him, reaching out to tickle his foot.

He chuckled, toes curling, but he managed not to wriggle, not even a little. It was hell being ticklish.

"Don't make me come over there and really tickle you, cowboy." Will sounded lazy and happy and just downright good.

"That would mean you had to move up off the ground, Ace. I wouldn't want you to strain anything." Dean grinned over, then started chuckling when Sadie came to inquire about why Will was on the ground.

Will let Sadie lick his nose, chuckling. "The only thing I'll get up for is food, or the possibility of a little necking."

Dean blinked, then shook his head, playing. "A little necking? Tell me, what's the good in that?"

"Well, a little usually leads to a lot." Wicked, that kid. Pure-D rotten to the core.

He knew his cheeks were heating, but he still managed to drag his gaze along Will's body, letting that long-legged cowboy know what he was thinking.

"This mean you're willing to wait on the ice cream?" Will's fingers traveled over his foot and up his calf, rubbing gently.

Oh. Homemade peach ice cream was almost as mouth-watering as that body. Of course, together they'd be.

Oh.

Damn.

His cheeks flared and his cock leapt, filling his jeans.

"What's that blush for, cowboy?" Trust Will to notice his damned red face.

"Hmm?" Best to go with distraction. There was no way in hell he'd be fessing up to having wicked daydreams about... what he was having wicked daydreams about. "Maybe I'm getting too much sun." He pulled down his hat a touch.

"Dean. I have seen you out in the sun all day long after losing your hat to some ornery mare and you just get more like a nut." Will snorted at his own joke. "Now what gives?"

"Well, I've been compared to lesser things, that's a fact." Dean grinned down. "This old man's just thinking thoughts, Ace. Nothing worth anteing up over."

"Oh, now." Will did sit up at that, leaning over to prop elbows on Dean's knees. "You let me decide that."

He reached out without even thinking much, stroked the edge of Will's chin, the brush of skin making him smile. "You're as curious as a cat and stubborn as a three dollar mule, you know that?"

"Somebody might have told me that a few times." It made Will smile, too, that touch, and the kid rubbed a rough stubbled cheek against him. "Still not letting it go."

"Just having less than pure thoughts about that body of yours, is all." He blushed darker, leg just rubbing a bit. "You'll forgive me that, I reckon?"

"Anything, cowboy. I just happen to like your impure thoughts." Will put a hand on his thigh, high up on the inside.

"Oh." He spread a little, sliding against that hand, hard enough to cut glass. "I was thinking peaches and you would taste mighty fine together. Little salt, little sweet. Just the thing."

"Peaches." A tiny frown creased Will's face. "We don't have any... oh. You mean the ice cream? Dean, you hound!" That hand squeezed.

If his cheeks got any redder, he'd be glowing. "Hush, you. I said it was nothing now." Still, he dared to lean forward, take a quick taste of lips, now didn't he?

The kiss he got back was hot and sweet and would melt anybody's ice cream. "I think it sounds like a damned fine idea."

Oh.

Dean blinked for a second, then took another kiss, moaning into those lips. Will's hands came up to push his hat off, sinking into his hair to hold him there and kiss him breathless.

He slid down, not even noticing how the lawn chair popped him in the back. Who would, belly-to-belly with the finest son of a bitch on earth. Damn.

That kiss left him purely lightheaded by the time Will pulled away. "Oh, damn, Dean. You do know how to kiss."

"You're no lightweight, Ace." He was breathing hard, wanting bad. That sweet package felt fine in his palm, the low noise Will made sounding good to his ears.

"Not when you're doing that I'm not." The breath of a chuckle moved against his mustache, and Will was kissing him again, hot and needy.

Those kisses were the sweetest damned things he'd ever had -- until they got hot and then, Lord have mercy! Sweet wasn't the way of it. Will was hungry and male and pure want all wrapped up in a pair of legs that were worth dreaming about.

Soon Will had them stretched out next to each other, hands finding his ass. Kid seemed focused on his ass. Not that he was going to complain when Will squeezed just that way. He rocked back into those hands a little, rubbed forward so that his palm was working Will's prick. Back and forth, just like riding, those kisses setting them at a nice canter.

Riding him like the cowboy he was, Will settled into the rhythm, hands moving on him, lips breaking off the kiss to find the spot under his ear that made him crazier than a horse with a burr under the saddle.

"Will..." He arched, head falling back, balls tight as all get out.

"Mmm." Will nibbled, licked, just went to town. "Where is that ice cream, cowboy?"

"In the cooler. Shit, Will, you keep that up this old man's gonna cream his jeans, I swear."

"I'd rather you creamed me out of mine." The bright chuckle made him smile, and Will left him with a kiss, going to the cooler to get the ice cream.

Dean sat up, ran his fingers through his hair. trying to catch his breath and clear his head. Damn, that man flitterpated him down deep.

The ice cream landed next to him on the ground, and Will started an impromptu striptease, wiggling out of shirt and jeans, sitting down to yank off those worn boots.

"Oh, damn..." He reached for the ice cream, pulling off the lid. "Will..."

"Yeah." Will was hard for him, ready, those long assed legs framing a hard cock and low swinging balls.

He stripped off his shirt and scooped up a bit of cream, bringing it over and popping it in his mouth before sliding his cold tongue along Will's shaft.

Sweet Christ.

"Oh, God. Jesus, Dean, you're gonna kill me." Will shook, legs going rock hard, cock pushing into his mouth.

He sucked until the peach flavor was gone, then repeated the action, swallowing Will deep.

Never gonna look at ice cream the same way again.

Never.

Will was just working it, hips rolling, begging for it. "That feels... God, Dean. Like nothing else, ever."

Over and over, ice cream, then Will, peach and man and oh, God, so sweet. So frigging **good**. His hand was working his own prick, jeans open, hips thrusting.

Before long, Will was crying out, pushing hard into his mouth and coming like a ton of bricks. He swallowed hard, moaning around Will's flesh, eyes rolling back in his head. This cowboy was going to **kill** him.

When Will pulled away and dropped to take his cock in that hot, hot mouth, he figured it would be worth it if he shuffled right off the mortal coil doing this with this man.

But not yet.

He arched into Will's mouth, body taut as a wire. Not quite yet.

Scrabbling with one hand, Will reached for the melting ice cream and pulled it over, dipping a fingerful out and onto his cock. Then sucking it off.

"Oh. Oh, God. Will..." His breath was sobbing in his chest and he thought his nutsac was going to pop. He hadn't been this horny since he was a colt fresh out of the gate.

"Mmm." Will pulled back just enough to get more ice cream on him. "Tastes so good, Dean. So good."

Dean whimpered, head rolling on the end of his neck, shoulders tense as steel. "Please. I need you."

"You've got me, Dean." Will set to sucking hard, fingers finding his balls and rolling them, one cold as Hell finger sliding against his hole, pushing in.

He came hard enough that his bones turned to dust, shot and shot until there wasn't an ounce of pleasure left in him.

The rough tongue that cleaned him sent sensation zinging through his spent cock, then Will was next to him, kissing him slow and easy. "God, that was good."

"Will, that left good in the dust." He chuckled and took another kiss, tasting peaches and him and Will and yeah, it was good.

Damned good.

"Yeah. Never had ice cream that appealed to me more." They lay together for a while, then Will rolled away, moving to grab a couple of spoons.

"No sense in wasting it, now that it's too soft to freeze it up again." Will grinned, handing him a spoon.

Dean took one and nodded. "I'm thinking our next winning? We ought to invest in a little freezer for the trailer."

He ate a spoonful, licking the cream off his mustache. "Either that or stock in Blue Bell."

Four

They were on the tail end of one of the worst weekends Will could remember in... well, maybe since he broke his leg.

Gypsy came up lame. The horse he drew in the bareback competition threw him off like a gnat off a bear's ass. Dean had taken a helluva spill when Blueboy stumbled in the warm ups, and didn't even get to compete.

Damn lucky the man wasn't hurt.

But they were both limping and nursing their pride and while neither of them were given to brooding, the silence around camp was more due to downright surliness than comfort. Damned time enough to change that, and Will would bet Dean wouldn't object to it either.

The night had cooled down a bit, the mosquitoes weren't bad enough to carry them off, and the stars were out, so Will grabbed a blanket and a couple of beers.

"Hey, cowboy. Let's hit the clearing and do some stargazing."

Dean looked like he was going to complain, when he just up and nodded. "Stargazing I can manage, Ace. I'm right behind you."

Will headed out and found them a stretch of ground that was almost flat, not too rocky. The blanket was a matter of seconds to rig and he lowered himself gingerly, stretching out and popping both beers open.

A series of snaps and pops followed Dean down, the cowboy's own personal drum section. "I tell you what, the ground keeps getting farther and farther away, the older I get."

"You think? I think it's not the age. It's the mileage." He grinned, handing over Dean's beer. "I feel like a three day bender that ended in a train wreck."

"Yeah? You're looking damn good for feeling so poorly." Dean upended the beer, throat working hard.

"Feeling better every minute." Damned if he wasn't. A long swig off his own beer helped. So did scooting close enough to Dean to feel the man's body heat.

Dean made a soft noise and leaned back, eyes trailing down his body. "You are one fine piece of man, Will. Makes a man need."

That slow burn that never seemed far off around Dean started in Will's belly, and he set the empty bottle aside, rolling up on one elbow to give Dean a long leisurely kiss.

"You do all right yourself, cowboy. Make me hungry."

Their lips came together again, this time with Dean driving the team, tongue sliding in for a long taste. Seemed like maybe Will wasn't the only one hungry. The sweet and sour taste of beer mixed with the deep, rich flavor he'd come to know as Dean, and his free hand came up to hold his lover in place, pulling that sweet lower lip with his teeth. God he loved to kiss that man.

One kiss melted into the other like a double-dip cone on an August afternoon. The flavors and sensations mingled, some slow and sweet, some harder-edged and salty with need, like finding a peanut in your coke. Salt and pepper and the tang of pure male, and Will ate it all up, letting Dean erase the tension in his back and the bruise on his ass and everything else. Time to just feel.

One of Dean's hands was resting on his belly, drawing slow and easy circles, around and around, petting him. His own hand went to Dean's neck, nails scraping along the skin there before he dug in and rubbed, knowing how Dean liked that. Goosebumps rose up under his fingers, and he smiled against Dean's lips.

His smile was licked, those eyes dark in the moonlight. Dean parted his lips to say something, then chuckled and pushed that so-clever-for-words tongue into his mouth. Didn't matter. He knew, and he agreed one hundred and ten percent. Will rolled a little, resting his weight on Dean so he could use both of his hands, tracing Dean's ribs, coming to rest on Dean's hips.

One of Dean's hands cupped his ass, the other walked fingers up his spine, sending little jolts of damned-good through him. "You're gonna miss the stars from there, Ace."

"Nah. This is much more interesting." Will nuzzled into the hollow of Dean's throat, sniffing, licking, just damned well wallowing in the man.

Dean moaned for him, a low rumbling, husky sound that his balls loved him to hear. Soft pants brushed his ear, Dean leaning up to whisper, "Damn, you'd make a dead man need."

"Well, I'm glad you're alive just the same."

His ass got a soft smack for that, and Will grinned again. Easy. That's what being with Dean was. Plain old easy. He took another kiss, feeling that mustache scrape and tickle. Dean worked those fingers under his t-shirt, working up toward his nipples to tweak and rub, reminding him how that mustache felt on other parts of him.

"Mmm." That shirt had to go, and while he was up

taking his off, he got hold of Dean's and pulled it off, too, urging the man up, then back down on the blanket. Such hot, hot skin.

Dean pulled him up a bit, mouth sliding over his chest, licking and nipping and tickling.

Yep. He remembered rightly about that mustache driving him purely crazy. It brushed and tickled and his nipples rose and his cock throbbed. He gave Dean a moan, letting his pleasure come through in the long sound.

That earned him a chuckle, a long lick, and that mouth fastening around one nipple and pulling right firm.

"Oh. Dean. I think I'm seeing the stars again." Corny? Maybe. True, though. He had to touch, down Dean's shoulders to his back, rubbing and circling.

Dean hummed against his chest, tongue sliding slow and easy as the cowboy worked across his skin.

They could go on all night if it wasn't for his jeans getting over tight, and him wanting the same taste of skin Dean was giving him, and Will scooted back again, shucking his Levi's, working on Dean's zipper while he was at it.

"Mmm... something's feeling good." Dean goosed him, grinning up into his eyes.

"Hell yes." He grinned, too, finding Dean's heat and hardness with his hands, cupping it, cradling it, before bending to lick at it.

"Oh! Shit, Will!" Dean's cry was sweet, hot like the swollen flesh throbbing under his tongue.

"Mmm." He let his tongue travel the underside, then came back up to catch the fluid at the tip before Will sucked Dean all the way in. So good.

Dean started jerking, moaning low and long, strong hands scrabbling on the blanket.

Too damned bad he wasn't up to anything acrobatic, or he'd get Dean to return the favor. As it was, he wasn't willing to let go of his prize, and Will sucked and licked and just ate the man up.

Soft words filled the air, his name and good and more and please, and then Dean was arching, warning him, fighting not to come. The Hell with that. He wanted it. Bad. Will sucked harder, fingers finding that fine ass and playing around the tight hole.

"Oh... Will..." Dean shuddered, cock pulsing as his mouth was filled, hole twitching under his finger.

Fuck. Salt and steel, his Dean, all sharp and bright. He tried not to let any go, licking his lips to catch any stray drops before nuzzling Dean's belly.

A trembling hand stroked his hair, Dean moaning low. "Damn. Just... damn."

"Yeah." He turned, rubbing his cheek against Dean's rough palm. "You taste so damned good, Dean. Better than Sunday dinner."

"Mmm... make me feel damned fine. C'mere, let me return the favor, give you what you need."

Yeah. He could do that. He moved up, wouldn't let Dean get him to straddle Dean's chest though, that strained the neck too much. Instead he knelt next to Dean's torso, let the man take his time. And stole a kiss while he was at it.

Dean shifted, mouth sliding down his belly, cheek rough against him as that tongue lapped at him. Fingers rolled his balls, cupped them as Dean took him in.

"Mmmnnnn. Dean." That was all he could manage, hard as he was, hard enough to pound nails into concrete. Hot and wet, Dean's mouth drove him to distraction.

Dean hummed, moving faster, hand sliding down to trace his crease.

He bucked, hips and belly straining, thigh muscles trembling. "Dean. Soon."

One finger pressed into him, Dean swallowing hard

around the head of his cock.

He grunted, hips snapping as everything in him came out, shooting down Dean's throat. He thought maybe he was gonna melt.

Dean sucked him dry, licking him clean before kissing his thigh. "Wow."

"I'll see your wow and raise you a Holy cow." Will flopped down next to Dean. "Just so you can't say I never learned poker."

Dean startled chuckling, laughter echoing beneath the stars. "I fold."

"God, I would sell my soul for a steak dinner." Will flopped back on the bed of the hotel room he'd actually paid for this time, and turned his head to grin at Dean. "One of these days I've gotta start winning enough to eat off."

Dean looked over at him, channel-flipping actually stopping. A few seconds passed and them Dean nodded. "You got yourself a deal, Ace. Go put on a clean shirt."

He chuckled. "You buying my soul, cowboy? 'Cause I'm serious. Hell, get me a T-bone and I'm yours forever."

"Yep. That's what I'm doing." Dean nodded again, voice serious as a heart attack. "You offered, I'm accepting. Get ready to go."

He peered at Dean a moment, then nodded once and rolled of the bed. Fair enough. He stripped off his shirt, ribs pulling like a sonofabitch and washed up at the sink, pulling out a clean white button up shirt. "So where are we going?"

"Texas Land and Cattle. There's one off the highway." Dean dug out a deep burgundy shirt and brushed it off, finding the grey ostriches in the suitcase and pulling them out too.

Oh, Hell. He loved that damned shirt. "Sounds good." All he had to do was run a comb through his hair and splash on a little Old Spice. He was wearing his best jeans anyway. They needed to do laundry in the worst way.

"It is." Dean was ready to go about five minutes before he was, slipping a wallet and a comb in one back pocket.

There was only one other thing he needed to do before they left and he walked right over to Dean to do it, putting a hand behind the man's neck and pulling him up for a kiss. Had to let Dean know how nice he looked. That mustache tickled, Dean's tongue sliding in for a soft sweet taste.

"Mmm. All this and steak, too." Patting Dean's butt, Will hightailed it for the door before he got caught up and forgot what he was about. "You ready?"

"Always." Dean patted Sadie's head and they headed to the truck, Dean whistling. The trailer was at the stockyard, so they didn't even have to unhitch, just get in and go.

The restaurant was a short drive -- three songs, maybe four, with traffic -- but the scent of broiling meat and fresh bread was perfect and Dean was looking fine standing in and among all that brass and dark wood.

Mouth watering. Both the smell of the food and the cowboy next to him. They got settled and got a beer and Will searched the menu for a t-bone and there it was. "Well, you sure do keep your end of a bargain."

"I do." Dean grinned wide and nodded. "I do. I'm thinking a nice t-bone sounds damned fine. Damned fine."

"I think you're right." They ordered t-bones, and Will

got the mashed potatoes and a big old pile of cole slaw with it. He could have a salad anytime. They argued the merits of medium rare versus medium well and neither of them won, which suited him just fine. Variety was good.

Dean ate a salad and they shared the dark bread. They chatted about the weekend's events, the horses. Dean looked good, eyes shining, relaxed, happy, young. It was the best look he could ask for outside of what they did behind closed doors, and Will soaked it up, smiling back, laughing and sharing bullshit stories.

Too much of their time was spent eyes on the prize. It was nice to think outside of that for a bit.

The steaks were perfect, the cheesecake that they shared for dessert was a perfect end. Dean was laughing over his coffee, flirting in that quiet, gentle way that would be so easy to miss.

Feeling pretty damned daring, Will nudged the toe of Dean's boot with his. "So, cowboy. Time for my end of the deal?"

Dean grinned, cheeks going pink. "I'm thinking I delivered, Ace. You're mine now."

Nodding, Will said very quietly, "Probably was anyway. But I figure it wouldn't hurt to prove it."

He got a nod. "No need to prove something that's flat out truth, Will."

That cracked him. "But it sure is fun to try."

"You think?" He got another playful grin, Dean finishing his coffee, wiping the cream off his mustache. "You ready?"

"Yeah." He left the tip, because when you weren't buying that was the polite thing, and they headed back for the hotel. Anticipation curled in his belly, hot and heavy. Last time they'd had a hotel they hadn't had any damned rubbers.

This time they did.

Dean was humming as they wandered out to the truck, the sound low and sweet, sort of sexy. "You want to drive, Ace?"

"Sure." He grinned like a kid and grabbed the keys, opening the passenger side for Dean. He did love that truck. "Thanks for dinner, Dean. That was the best damned steak in a long time."

"It was my pleasure." Dean hopped up, giving him a shot of that sweet, tight ass sliding into the seat.

Anticipation was fast turning into hard desire, but there was no rush. It was nice to ache sometimes. "Well, mine, too. I swear that cheesecake was almost better than the steak."

He eased the out of the parking lot, following Dean's directions back to the hotel, an idea coming upon them when they parked.

"Come on, cowboy. We need to get to stage two." He winked, sauntering ahead of Dean and letting them in.

"Stage two?" Dean followed behind, voice husky and edged with a sweet wanting.

"Yeah. You dined me. Now we go dancing." The tiny clock between the beds had a radio, and Will turned it on, flipping stations until the sweet strains of Walking After Midnight came in clear and sharp.

"C'mere, you."

The smile he got could have lit up the Mesquite Rodeo Arena.

Dean moved into his arms, just like that cowboy belonged there.

Which he did, now, didn't he? Will didn't bother with a waltz, just commenced to polishing his belt buckle on Dean's belly. They swayed in time to the music, his arms coming up to hold Dean close, fitting together like a jigsaw puzzle.

Dean hummed soft, the sound tickling his shoulder

as that warm cheek settled on his shoulder, strong hands framing his ass.

Life was good. Real good. The music changed, something newer that he didn't recognize, but still slow enough to dance close to, and they turned in lazy circles, feet barely moving.

He could feel Dean's breath, sliding over his throat, lips tracing slow circles so softly he thought he was imagining them at first. His own breath stirred Dean's hair, his hands squeezed rhythmically at Dean's ass, and Will tilted his head to let Dean at more of his skin.

Their dancing started to have less and less to do with the radio and more to do with tongues on skin and denim rubbing denim. Soft moans. Quiet, breathless kisses.

They'd better dance closer to the bed, he figured, because the way his knees were getting all sponge-y they were just gonna topple over. Will started working the buttons of Dean's shirt, letting go of that fine ass with reluctance, but wanting skin.

Dean was working his neck, licking and nibbling, hands sliding between them to pop open his belt.

Felt good, both the kisses and the freedom from the pressure of his jeans as they opened. He got Dean's shirt off, hands smoothing over that sleek back, feeling the scars under his fingers that always spoke to him of strength and pure grit.

"Mmm... 's good." The words were muffled, Dean unbuttoning his shirt, exploring his chest, slow and quiet and sure.

"Yeah. Real good." He did some nuzzling and licking himself, going for Dean's buckle and zipper.

They were breathing harder, Dean's mustache sliding over his nipple, making it hard, even as Dean cupped his cock, thumb tracing the shaft.

"Oh, man." Rolling his hips and holding on, Will let

the pleasure slide through him, let it settle deep in his gut. "We've got a bed, cowboy. Want you to do me this time."

"Mmm... Yeah. I can manage that." The hand against him tightened as Dean moaned. "Want you"

"Yeah. Time to move on to stage three." He chuckled and moaned at the same time, and damned if his head wasn't gonna just explode with pleasure and need.

Dean laughed, teeth scraping his nipple. "Three-two-one, blast off?"

"Something like that." Dean's hair was thick and springy, and it felt good between his fingers. Will massaged Dean's scalp, his neck and shoulders. "Want you naked, Dean. So we need to get rid of the boots."

"You're damned practical when it comes to what we need, Ace. Damned good quality to have in a man."

"You know it. You're the brawn. I'm the brains." He took one last kiss before shoving Dean back against the bed, bending to pull the man's boots off.

Between them and their laughter and their kisses, they managed to get naked and horizontal and in the bed. Dean was pressed up close, taking one kiss after another, fingers sliding along his spine.

Felt better than anything, being with Dean. Got his heart beating faster than an eight second ride on a ninety point horse. That mustache tickled like crazy, moving over his lips and chin and throat, making him squirm.

Dean hummed, one hand stroking his prick, the other teasing at the top of his cleft, drawing circles over and over. Maddening. The man was just gonna kill him. He drew some circles of his own, on Dean's back and then his chest, finding the tiny nipples there and tugging.

That got him a groan, those fingers sliding down to circle his entrance, teasing and testing the ring of muscles.

"The table, Dean. I laid the stuff out before we left." He was just gasping, slow and steady becoming hot and needy.

Dean lifted up, reaching over him to grab the lube. A low sound left Dean and those eyes were hot as they reappeared. "Turn over on your side, Will. There's a mirror on the chest of drawers. We can watch."

"Damn, you have good ideas." Good didn't even begin to cover it, but he would leave it at that. Will rolled, coming to rest on his side, facing the mirror. He could see Dean behind him, looking at him so hot, and everything in him jumped right to attention. His cock just throbbed. "Oh damn."

"Yeah. Damn." Dean fiddled for a second and then those hot fingers traced his hole, slick and sure. Those granite eyes shone for him, teeth scraping his shoulder as Dean slid one finger deep.

The touch made him arch his back, made him open right up, and he held Dean's eyes in the mirror, watching the man watch him. One of the hottest things he'd ever done.

Dean took his sweet time, moving from one finger to two so easy he almost didn't notice. A moan sounded, Dean's lips beneath his ear. "Shit, cowboy. You are so fine. Feel so good to me."

"Good." So easy, so right. "'Cause you feel like Heaven, Dean." He blushed a little, saying something so corny with Dean staring right at him like that, but it was nothing but the truth.

He couldn't touch Dean much from the angle he was at, but he could put on a show, so he grabbed his own cock and started stroking.

"Oh... Will..." Dean shuddered behind him, hard prick sliding wet-tipped along his thigh. Those fingers pressed deep, sparking need as they rubbed inside him.

"Can't... can't take much more Dean. You'd better hurry up." Will pushed back onto Dean's fingers, forward into his hand, panting worse than a hot dog.

"Thank God." Dean's forehead rested on his shoulder, the crinkle of the rubber just drawing the need out. Then it was Dean, thick and sure, pushing into him, hand on his hip and pulling him close.

The mirror showed them locked close together, looking like they shared skin, Dean's hand dark against the skin of his hip and thigh, skin that never saw the sun.

Will moaned, and arched his head back, searching for Dean's mouth. "Dean..."

"Yes." Dean pushed deep, mouth covering his in a needy kiss, their bodies jerking together harder and faster.

So good. He could feel it rising in his spine, pleasure about to burst right out of him, and he pushed back hard, taking Dean in so far, feeling the muscles in his belly start to clench.

Dean's fingers twined with his, working his cock in time with those thrusts. Oh, God. He could see it, when the kiss ended, see their joined hands on his cock and Will moaned, loud and long, spunk spilling out of him in gut wrenching bursts.

"Oh, sweet Jesus. Will..." Dean's words sounded like a prayer, hips jerking furiously for a few, long moments before the warm body shook behind him.

"Oh. Oh, yeah." They just sorta went limp, both of them, sinking into each other. Nothing had ever felt like that. Nothing.

Dean pulled out, slow and easy, getting rid of the rubber and wiping them both up, before cuddling in close, arm holding him tight.

Grinning sleepily, he met Dean's eyes in the mirror once more. "That was better than a steak dinner. 'Course, the whole evening was a fine thing. Thank you."

He got a soft, slow smile. "Oh, I think we're both damned lucky, Ace."

"Yeah." They were. It worked both ways. He might have sold his soul for that steak dinner, but Dean was the one who bought it.

Damned lucky.

Five

There was nothing to be upset about.

Nope.

Not a damned thing.

Just because that fella from St. Louis was playing pool with Dean, and flirting with him, and Will wanted to strangle the man, didn't mean Dean was flirting back. Even if it looked like it. Dean was just being nice. Neighborly. Unwilling to make the guy feel unwelcome.

Will was going to kill him.

Didn't help that Dean was wearing that maroon shirt that he liked so much. Or those new jeans that framed that fine ass just so.

Or that Dean was laughing at the bastard's terrible jokes.

Will tried to ignore it. He really did. Wasn't like him to get pissy about a man having a good time, and what Dean did to have fun was his own business, full stop. But damn. Jealousy had never taken him like that, ever, hard and deep in his gut. His jaw hurt he was gritting his teeth so hard.

Once or twice he caught Dean's eyes on him, sure and quiet, steady sort of, then they'd be gone again, caught answering the bartender's questions or taking his next shot.

Finally he heard the man ask Dean if maybe Dean wouldn't want to go out for a walk, maybe a few beers somewhere else.

Oh, now. He knew Dean was going to say no. Knew it. But damned if that didn't make him see red, anyway. That cowboy was his. That fine ass? All his, too.

Will got up and sauntered over, hooking his thumbs in his belt loops. "You ready to go?"

Dean gave him a look, then nodded. "Sorry, pal, but it's time to mosey. You have a good one, yeah?"

Then, without another comment, Dean paid their tab and led him out of the bar.

Will turned on one boot heel and followed, steaming gently. If Dean gave him one bit of shit for being rude, he was gonna boil right over like a too full cobbler.

Dean tossed him the truck keys in the parking lot, not acting pissed or being a bitch, just walking toward the pickup.

They made it to the truck, which was just out of the range of the lights on either side of the bar door. Then he snapped. Will didn't even think to look around, just grabbed Dean and pushed him up against the side of the truck, kissing him hard.

Dean gasped, then opened up to him, hands hard on his hips and pulling them tight together.

Oh. Damn. So good. That was what he needed. Dean under his hands, under his lips. He went from mouth to neck, setting his teeth to Dean's throat, nuzzling beneath the collar of Dean's shirt to suck up a mark.

Dean made a low, sharp sound, then pushed him away. "Not here. Not like this. Come to the room, Will. Gonna make me embarrass myself."

God. He wanted to just keep going, shove Dean in the truck and keep on keeping on. But the room could be good, too. Get Dean naked and have that ass all to himself.

Forehead against Dean's, Will nodded. "Okay, cowboy. We'll play it your way."

"Fuck." Dean took another kiss, tongue pushing into his mouth, proving how hungry, how wanting his cowboy was.

No more than he was. Will kissed back, grabbing Dean's ass, grinding against him. Dean's moustache rubbed his cheek, then his throat, and Will moaned, loving it. Dean's teeth scraped across the skin of his throat, sharp and hot. He tilted his head back, letting Dean have him. It was only fair. He wanted. Oh, damn, he wanted.

Dean made a low sound, almost a growl, lips fastening on his throat, skin pulled sharply.

"Dean!" That made him buck like the last bronc that threw him, hands sliding up Dean's back to hold that mouth in place, hard as a damned rock in his jeans.

Needing.

His throat was aching by the time Dean lifted his head, eyes hot. "Truck. I need. Get in the truck, please?"

"Yeah." The keys were still in his hand, totally forgotten, and he unlocked the cab so they could pile in together, Will reaching for Dean again as soon as they were inside.

"Shit, cowboy. Made me crazy in there."

"Playing pool?" Dean pushed right into his arms, that pretty shirt soft against his hands.

He reached for the buttons of that shirt, wanting to see Dean's skin framed by it. "Playing with that jerk."

"You mean the kid from St. Louis? Shit, he's not you, Will." Dean leaned back a little, let him open his shirt.

"No. And you're with me." There. Chest. Dean's nipples, which just called to him, and he had to bend down and taste them, leaving a dark mark above one.

"Hell, yes. Nowhere else I'd rather be." Dean arched, nipples hard and hot, hands clumsy and grasping against his shoulders.

"Good." He was still feeling pretty possessive, hot in his belly, making him want to bite and lick and suck. It was new, that feeling, new having someone he gave a damn about, but good. He licked at Dean's other nipple, hand covering Dean's cock through his jeans.

Dean nodded, stretched a little, offering him a long line of skin.

Oh. Pretty. So pretty. Will squeezed and licked and nibbled and left a scattering of fine bruises. He was probably squashing the Hell out of the man, but he didn't care.

"Shit, Will. Feels... feels damned good." Dean's hips rocked up toward his hand, head falling back.

"Love the way you taste, Dean. Love how hot you are. Just... couldn't stand the thought of you and that yahoo." The button of Dean's jeans gave under his hand, and he reached in, getting under the briefs to find Dean's cock.

"Fuck, Will." Dean lifted his head, eyes meeting his own. "Don't you know I'm yours?"

Oh. Oh damn. "I know, Dean. 'Cause I'm yours just as right and tight. But I just... I'm sorry."

"Shush. We'll chat on it later. Right now?" Those eyes twinkled, chin raising, showing the dark mark on Dean's throat. "You make sure that yahoo knows I'm taken."

"God, yeah. Mine, cowboy. All mine." He traced each mark with his lips, pulling on Dean's cock, loving how it felt in his hand.

Dean gave him one soft noise after another, all warm and wanting and happy. His. Pushing, pulling and bending, Will took Dean's cock in his mouth, sucking hard. His.

"Oh! Will!" Dean bucked, fingers digging into the

upholstery, boots planted on the floorboard.

"Mmm." Greedy, that's what he was. He licked at the slit, savoring the flavor, inhaling deeply. His Dean.

"Will. God. Gonna... Not gonna take long..." Dean's fingers were surprisingly soft in his hair.

Good. He sucked harder, hand brushing Dean's balls through the open zipper, tongue running up the ridge underneath. He wanted to make Dean crazy. Wanted to hear his name on Dean's lips as he came.

"Oh, sweet lord..." Dean bucked, cock twitching, jumping on his tongue as Dean spilled. "Yours, Will. Oh. Yours."

Dean tasted bittersalty and scalding hot, and Will swallowed every bit, licking Dean clean. "Mine. Damn, Dean. Mine."

"Yeah. Yours and you're mine." Dean shivered, fingers stroking his hair. "Not looking to share."

"Good." He crawled back up, gave Dean a kiss that was both possessive and apologetic. "Neither am I."

"Good." Dean smiled at him. "Now. That's settled. Take me to the hotel and take my ass?" Oh, so wicked.

"Hell, yes." He smiled back, and settled in the driver's seat, heading back to the hotel at a good clip.

There was nothing to be upset about. Not a thing in the world, now he had Dean.

Well, now. Will had to say dinner had gone damned well indeed. Life was good, and they were living high, having rented one of those cabin type motel rooms with a little kitchenette.

After a trip to the store, Will set to making homemade fried chicken, and biscuits and gravy, and a real pie, not a thrown together campfire cobbler. Apple, with the flaky crust and all.

From the remains, which were few, Will would say it was a hit. And after Dean did the dishes and they had a bit of a nap, Will was looking to get his reward for good behavior.

'Course, Dean was still asleep. Which might be a problem if he wanted audience participation.

Will rolled over, settling close, letting one hand come to rest on Dean's waist as he leaned in to nuzzle the spot just below Dean's chin that tickled like a son-of-a-bitch. Dean snorted a little, one arm reaching out to pull him close, settle him. Sort of like the cowboy did Sadie when she was restless, but a little more up close and personal.

Well, shit. Will moved even closer, plastering up against Dean's side, sliding one leg over both of Dean's. Then he dug his fingers into Dean's ribs and tickled.

Dean bucked like a Brahma, but Will just held on, riding it out until those eyes caught hold of him, one eyebrow raising. "You wanting something, Ace?"

"Nah. Just thought I'd practice for this weekend." He grinned, pecking a kiss on the end of Dean's nose.

Dean's laughter tickled him and those hands slid down his ass to goose him. "You look to be riding just fine, cowboy."

Laughing with Dean was easy as falling off a calf riding backwards. "I've got the finest mount here this side of Cheyenne."

"Reckon I'm a sight better than a harelipped mule, I do." Dean grinned and started drawing tracks along the skin of his lower back.

"Mmm." Damn that man had fine hands. "A damn sight better, Dean. Oh. There." Dean hit that spot, right at the top of his ass, and Will felt it zing right up his spine.

"Here?" Oh, that voice was as wicked as a Louisiana

whore's as Dean played the nerves, stroking again and again.

"Yeah." His voice broke on the word, and he moved into Dean's touch, loving the feel of them together. Loving the way they fit.

"Turn over, Will." Dean's voice was husky and, when Will settled on his belly, Dean scooted down, that mustache sliding over those tingling nerves.

"Oh. Oh, God." The scrape and tickle maddened him, made his whole body stand up and salute the flag, and Will just moaned and humped the sheets.

The touch of a wet tongue, hot as a branding iron, joined in the fray, sparking the nerves along his spine like it was the Fourth of July. The man was going to kill him. Will flailed, needing something, God knew what. Well, it could have been one of any number of things. Dean's mouth, Dean's fingers. Dean's cock.

"Please. Dean. Just... God."

The chuckle tickled, driving him batshit crazy, but then those thumbs spread him open and... Oh. Oh. Oh, sweet Jesus. Oh.

That tongue moved, soft and slow and so hot.

Oh.

Somewhere in there his brain went fuzzy. No one had ever done anything like that to him before. The mustache, Dean's lips and tongue, the feeling of those rough hands spreading him wide, they all conspired to make him a gibbering idiot.

Then that tongue slid over him, tracing his hole and oh, God. God. Dean was pushing in, the motion slow and easy, careful, those hands holding him and keeping him together.

All he could do was let it happen, let Dean have him. Let Dean take him places he never thought to see. He took up great fistfuls of the sheets, pushing up and back. Dean just keep spurring him higher, farther, tongue teaching him things he didn't know to look into learning.

He was gonna explode like a box of dynamite. Will bucked and moaned and groaned, amazed at himself for the things he said.

Finally he heard himself make some sense. "Dean. Damn it. In me."

One thing he could say for his cowboy. Dean wasn't slow on the draw, spreading him and pushing two slick fingers in deep. "Will..."

"Yeah. Now. Dean." He propped himself up, spreading his legs wide, ass waving in the air like a damned bitch in heat, but he was so ready. "Now."

The hard, hot pressure of Dean filling him was as welcome as rain on the desert, the strokes hard and deep, giving him what he needed.

The need was fierce, too, driven by Dean's hot touches, hotter kisses, and Will put a hand down to his cock, pulling desperately. The ride had never been better.

"Soon, Will. Damn. So hot. Soon." The whispered words brushed over his skin, Dean's lips following.

Hot wasn't going to begin to cover it. Burning up was what he was. The stretch and burn where Dean fit into him felt so deep and good and right, and Will let each thrust rock him right to the core.

Then Dean bucked, sliding right over that spot where heaven met earth, sending shockwaves through him.

That was all he could take. Will hollered, hips pushing, back arching like to snap in two, coming hard enough to see fireworks on his closed eyelids.

When the sparkles faded, Dean was slowly pulling out of him, dropping soft kisses on his shoulders.

"Mmhhnn." Yeah. That came out well.

Dean nodded, chuckling against his skin. "No shit."

He managed to turn, with a little help from Dean,

and get a real kiss, lip to lip. And he thought dinner went well? That was one helluva dessert.

Goddamn it was hot. Hot, hot, and fucking hot, with a side of hot.

Will wasn't one for bitching about things he couldn't help. And heaven knew he had lived in what some people called the northern tip of Hell. But he just couldn't settle.

They'd left Gypsy and Blue at the rodeo grounds, because they had a nice barn there with misters and fans. Sadie was right under the little window unit, and she was still panting. And Will was naked on the hotel bed with a bucket of ice from the icemaker, waiting while Dean took a shower.

Good thing they didn't have to worry about using up all the **cold** water.

"I tell you what, Ace, it's hotter than the inside of a dog's mouth." Dean came sauntering in, shaking his head. "We might have to go to the movies tomorrow just to cool off."

"I hear ya." Oh, that wasn't helping at all, Dean with little drops of water all over and a towel around his waist. Made him even hotter. Will grabbed for the nearest ice cube, rubbing it along his neck.

Dean's eyes followed the ice, tongue sliding out to brush the edge of that mustache. "That feel good?"

"You know it does." He grinned, that look lighting a fire in his belly. "Want some?"

"Yeah," Dean walked over, took a piece of ice and placed it between his lips, then bent and circled one nipple, leaving an icy trail.

"Oh!" Damn, sometimes Dean surprised the heck

out of him, and didn't that speak well for a little age and experience? Will arched, nipple drawing up tight, shivering a little. Nice.

Dean grinned, ice and mustache and water traveling along his ribs.

His legs drew up, hands coming up to touch Dean's hair, rubbing over the short strands. He was cold and hot all at once, and the feeling was something else. Damn.

"Feels good, cowboy."

"Tastes pretty fine, too." Dean took another piece of ice, mouth moving over his belly.

"Yeah?" Will grinned, letting go of Dean with one hand to reach for more ice, trailing a piece down Dean's back. "Not exactly cooling me off."

Dean arched, the water catching the ropy lines of the scars, tricking down in scattered patterns. "Oh, that feels good. Fine."

Those scars fascinated him, called his fingers, and Will rubbed over them, letting the water dry under his touch. "It sure does."

Another piece of ice was snatched, then a cold suction wrapped around his prick, the act sudden, surprising.

It damn near deflated him for a minute, but then it kicked him into overdrive. Will shouted, trying to curl around Dean, trying to get more of that hot, hot mouth with the freezing jolt of the ice. "Dean! Oh, fuck."

Dean chuckled, hand cupping his ass, encouraging his motions, that hot and cold tongue driving him wild.

"Oh. Oh." He was shorting out, just not able to do a damned thing for Dean, even though he wanted to. His hands just went all clumsy and his hips pumped and Will watched that salt and pepper head move on him, figuring he was about to go up in flames.

The slick slide of Dean's tongue, the brush of mustache, the fading chill of the ice -- it was all working against him. So were those fingers under his ass, and the brush of Dean's arms on his thighs, making the hairs there stand up. God, he was losing it.

He was spread, Dean's fingers brushing his hole, teasing and tempting.

"Fuck!" Will bucked and rolled, heat coming up inside to rival the heat outside, pouring into Dean's mouth. Damn, that cowboy did him up right, and the sweat was drying, cooling him off nicely.

"Mmm... fine ride there, Ace." Dean kissed the tip of his cock, humming low.

"Uh huh." Sure, now his own tongue wouldn't work worth a damn, either. Will grinned down, hands kicking back into order, at least, so he could pet Dean's shoulders.

Dean settled, close enough to be friendly, far enough away that the heat wasn't unbearable. "Hope that ice machine's working good."

"So do I. I can think of a thousand things to do with it now." Oh, there was his mouth and brain connecting.

Dean chuckled. "Oh, I'm thinking that this is gonna be the best heat wave ever."

"You think?" He grinned, dipping his fingers in the quickly melting ice in the bucket and drawing a pattern on Dean's arm.

Dean shivered, arms raising up, belly rippling. "Oh, I think, yessir."

Oh, that belly was so hot. All of Dean was, but he had an inspiration thinking of all of Dean's hot places. He took up a piece of ice and reached, turning Dean onto his belly, starting at the base of Dean's neck and tracing scars.

"Oh..." Oh, now that sound? That sound was pure sex and need and want all wrapped up tight together.

That was inspiring. The tiny chip of ice wasn't going

to do it, though, so Will got another, rubbing it over each bump of spine, each raised piece of flesh.

"I never... shit, Ace, I swear. I never thought anybody could make them seem sexy."

"Mmm. Everything about you is sexy, Dean." That was only the truth, and Will leaned down and licked at the moisture he'd left on Dean's back, dragging his tongue over the scars.

Dean just moaned, hips shifting, rocking into the sheets, tight ass moving so pretty. That ass... he had plans for that ass. Will grabbed more ice, running it right down the center of Dean's back and letting it melt at the top of Dean's crease.

"Will..." Dean's legs parted just pretty, water sliding down.

"Yeah. Oh, Dean. Damn, old man, you're something else." He slipped his wet fingers between Dean's cheeks, pushing lightly, before bending to lick where fingers and ice had been. Dean's ass? Gave him palpitations.

Dean took a deep shuddering breath, sheets creaking as those hands tightened.

Perfect. More ice, more licking, both sliding in to find Dean's tight little hole, and Will pushed the ice against it with his tongue, listening for Dean's reaction. His own cock twitched back to life, and he rubbed on Dean's leg, moaning a little.

"Sweet fuck!" Dean jerked, cry harsh and turned on, hips tilting up, entire body begging.

God, that dragged Dean's leg against his prick, and he was trying for suave? Too bad it wasn't gonna work. Will gave up on the ice, spreading Dean's cheeks with his thumbs and licking and sucking, pushing his tongue right in.

"Oh, Will. Shit. Need. So hot." Rocking, moaning, Dean was like a two-dollar pistol in his hands.

He wasn't noticing the heat anymore, at least not anything but Dean's heat under his hands and mouth. God, Dean made him crazy, made him want to taste and touch and smell everything. He kept working that sweet butt, thumbs pushing into the muscles, lips and tongue working the hole, happy as a clam.

"Close. Close, Will. Oh, fuck. Please." Oh. Oh, begging. Begging in that husky, raw East Texas drawl.

He gave Dean what he needed, sliding one hand under to play those drawn up balls, that hot as a brand cock, teasing and petting and stroking. He kept working Dean until he was ready to go off again, too, humping hard, panting, sweat dripping on Dean's skin, a lot wetter than the melting ice had ever been.

Dean jerked, grunted, bucked into his hand like a bronco out of the gate, seed spraying.

"Uhn." Oh, God. The scent, the feel of Dean's ass clenching around him, that was too much, and he was damned glad he was young, because coming twice in such a short time might kill him in this heat.

Dean slumped down, moaning low. "Shit, Marthy, that was... Damn."

That? Was an understatement. Will grinned, flopping close to Dean, feeling their sweat fuse them together. "Hell, yes. We'll need to take another shower now. Oh, damn."

What a horrible thing.

Dean chuckled. "Hell, Ace, we'll line that mother with towels and fill it up and sleep there."

"Oh, yeah. Now that sounds like a plan." He chuckled, patting Dean's butt. "I'll make the lemonade."

"I'll run the water."

They moved, finally, kissing clumsily, both a little sleepy, but determined to get cooled off before they collapsed.

Heat waves were a bitch, and Lord didn't he know that? But sharing anything, including a summer hot enough to cook eggs on the sidewalk, with Dean? Made it all worthwhile.

Six

Will hung up the payphone and stared at it for a minute. Then he shook it off and headed back to the diner, where Dean and a plate of apple pie and ice cream waited for him.

He slid into the booth across from Dean, smiling as the man looked up, one eyebrow rising. "Mom's fine. Dad says nothing got busted but her pride."

He'd checked his messages on the last leg of the trip and there'd been one from his dad saying his mother had taken a spill, but no one answered the damned phone. So at the next stop he tried again. Thank God it was all good.

"Good to hear it. Getting old's hell on the bones." Dean was drinking a cup of coffee, a pattern of random numbers scribbled on the paper napkin.

"Yeah." Will dug into his pie. The ice cream was a little soft, but not bad. "Dad says Roy's going to be in Fort Worth this weekend. Wants to meet for dinner."

"Yeah? What brings him out here?"

"Well, since mom's down in the back, dad decided not to come to the cattleman's thing he was up for. Roy's going to come out in his place." Will looked at Dean from under his lashes. "I'd like it if you'd come and meet him."

"Yeah?" Dean nodded, finishing his coffee and putting the cup down. "I'd cotton up to that, sure. We'd best hit a laundry, though. I got nothing clean worth meeting family in."

"I don't either." He grinned, licking sugar off his upper lip. "I tell ya, Dean, I got a whiff of myself this morning and figured we needed to wash some things."

"Well, now. There you go." Dean laughed, eyes watching his tongue. "I'm thinking there's a washing machine in that motel we're in. We stop and buy some Cokes, we oughta get some quarters."

"Sounds good." Well, that was easy. The pie was gone too soon, though, for anything as good as it was, and Will ran a finger around the plate, scooping up crumbs and sucking them off his finger.

"So... your brother? Y'all real close?" Dean patted his shirt pocket, the habit from years of smoking.

"Yeah. Well, not in the last year or so, since I started the circuit up again. But before." Will nodded. "He was the biggest help when I was laid up."

"Sounds like good people." Dean took the ticket and paid the tab. "While we're this far north, we ought to run out, check on Daddy, see the land."

"Works for me." They headed for the truck. "You think doing some laundry will earn us the right to some beer and a game of pool later on?"

"I sure as shit hope so. I need to win that ten spot back from you from last time." Dean grinned.

Once they were in the truck's cab, Will reached over and gave Dean's thigh a squeeze. "Think you'll like Roy."

"I reckon I will. After all, I've met Mrs. Benton's younger boy and he's fine. Just fine."

Chuckling, he gave Dean a sideways look and a

squeeze higher up a bit. "Well, I'm hoping you don't like him that much."

"I'm thinking that won't be an issue." Dean's thighs parted for him, voice going a little husky.

"You don't think so? Everyone always says Roy's better looking than I am. Not so gangly." He was teasing, but he couldn't help it. At least they weren't moving yet.

"Gangly?" Dean turned, looked him up and down, those grey eyes hot as all get out. "Ace, there isn't a man walking can scratch my itch like you can."

Oh, and didn't that make him hot and bothered. Laundry might have to wait a bit. He inched his way up to Dean's fly, pressing against the heavy ridge under it. "Good. Roy wouldn't do you much good that way, anyway."

Dean's eyes rolled, tongue sliding out to wet those lips. "I ain't worried on your brother, Will."

"Yeah? What are you worried about?" The top button of Dean's jeans gave way under his fingers, and Will dipped down below the waistband, just searching.

"About those hands of yours driving me plumb insane..." Dean's lips parted, hat tipped down a little.

Now that? Was just something, Dean's eyes glinting at him from under the brim of his hat. Will took his own hat off, dropping it on the dashboard before unzipping Dean's jeans all the way. "Wait until you see what my mouth is gonna do."

Oh, that look? Pure lust. Damn. Dean's body rippled, shifted on the seat.

Made it worth doing it in public, which he never would have thought on until now. He looked around carefully before bending down, one hand on the steering wheel to keep his head from bumping, and licking at the tip of Dean's cock.

"Will..." Dean sounded stunned and shocked and

completely turned on, hand falling on his shoulder.

"Mmmhmm." The scent of Dean owed nothing to dirty laundry. It was pure and male and deep, teasing him. The taste was even better, and Will dipped his tongue into the slit of Dean's cock, pulling up moisture.

"Oh. Oh, damn. Will, I haven't ever... Not like this." Dean pushed up, gasping, cock hard and throbbing in his lips.

Yeah. God, that catch in Dean's voice made him crazy, well even more crazy than he was if he was going down on Dean in the truck in a parking lot for God's sake. He closed his lips tight around Dean, sucking and licking, eyes closed and cheeks hollowed.

Dean was hot as August, hips moving, that hand on his shoulder opening and closing convulsively.

He could feel the beat of Dean's pulse, could hear Dean's stifled noises. They drove him on, made him open his throat, trying to get all the way down.

"Oh. Oh, sweet Christ. Will. Gonna. Fuck. Soon." The words were low, bit out, damn near growled.

Hell, yes. He wanted it. Bad. Will sucked harder, fingers sliding into Dean's jeans to touch the base of that sweet cock, stroking in time.

Dean grunted, cock jumping, salty heat pouring into his lips just like that.

God, he loved that. Loved that taste. Love the way Dean's thighs tightened under him, the way Dean shook. Will licked his lips, sitting up and smiling.

"You. I. Damn." Dean looked stunned. Melted, but stunned. "We need to go to the hotel. We can do laundry tonight."

"Okay." Yeah, they needed the hotel. Immediately if not sooner. Will was gonna pop right in his jeans.

Dean pulled out of the parking lot, just booking it, cheeks still flushed.

"Now, don't get us a ticket, cowboy." He was just wiggling, shifting.

"I'm thinking that's not what I'm wanting to get, Ace." Those eyes blazed at him. "Not at all."

Oh, God. "Stop that, or I'll be humping my hand right here in the truck, old man." He would, too. Just watch.

Dean groaned, shook his head. "No, sir. That's mine, Will. All mine."

"Yours." He was panting, cheeks hot, throat tight. Fuck.

They made the hotel in record time, Dean right behind him as they got out of the truck, pushing them to get in the room. Will fumbled with the old-fashioned key, finally getting the door open in a rush and running in.

Dean didn't play, just hustled him over to the bed, mouth crashing down on his like a ton of bricks. Good. So good. Will arched against him, rubbing, trying to get some relief. Something. Anything.

His belt buckle got torn open, Dean's fingers rough, clumsy, fishing his cock right out before his cowboy hit the floor, sucking him in deep.

"Oh! Oh, Dean. God." He was shaking, hips just rocking, hands coming to pet Dean's shoulders, his hair, knocking off the hat Dean hadn't managed to hang by the door. His balls drew up, his belly quivered, and Will knew he was gonna blow soon.

Dean hummed, took him down to the base, mouth working hard, head just bobbing.

Will panted, wriggled, humped for all he was worth, and finally he just lost it, coming hard into Dean's waiting mouth. Holy hell. Dean groaned, tongue still sliding, stroking.

"Oh, cowboy. Blow my mind." Will flopped back on the bed, swimmy eyes trained on the ceiling.

Dean crawled up, cheek on his belly. "Damn."

"Yeah. You just... you're something else." He stroked Dean's face, his neck, idly drawing patterns. He loved this man something fierce.

"You looking forward to introducing me to your people?"

Was he? He was so proud of Dean he might bust. Of course he was. "I can't wait. They're gonna love you."

Dean grinned. "Daddy's looking forward to meeting you, too, Ace. He's a little addled, so he might not remember you long, but I told him about you."

That was just so damned sad. He could see the hurt in Dean when he talked about it. "I'm glad I get to meet him, cowboy."

"Me, too." Dean's mustache brushed over his skin. "Damn, you make me happy."

"Same here, Dean. Same here." So when it came down to it? He really didn't care what his family thought. He hoped they liked Dean, because it would make it a heck of a lot easier. But if they didn't? He still wasn't letting go.

Not one damned bit.

"He's too old for you."

"What?" Will's forkful of banana cream pie plopped back on his plate, wobbling like crazy. He stared at Roy, just pop-eyed. "What the hell are you talking about?"

"He's a real nice fella. He's got a way about him, and I like how he is with you. But he's too old for you, Will."

"Bullshit." Snorting inelegantly, Will looked to make sure Dean wasn't on his way back from the bathroom. "He's just right."

"No, he's not." Goddamn, but Roy had that stubborn look on his face. That one that had gotten Will through rehab for his leg, like it or not. "His career is on the downslide, Will. Yours is just starting. You stay with him, he'll be wanting to settle, wanting you to stay with him."

"He'd never ask me to do something I didn't want to, Roy."

Roy had seemed to get along with Dean so well, laughing at the jokes, rubbing elbows with him just fine, so this caught him off guard like a sucker punch to the breadbasket. Hell, he figured he'd be spitting biscuits and pot roast any minute.

"That's what you say now. But a man gets to where he wants a place of his own, Will. You'll see."

"Fuck you, Roy."

Roy went red, mouth opening, but it snapped shut and Will looked over his shoulder to see Dean walking toward them, smiling at him like he hung the moon.

No way was Dean too old for him. Roy'd see in time.

He just knew it.

Will didn't really mean to slam things around. Lord knew Dean didn't deserve his foul mood, hadn't earned it. Roy was the one he was downright peeved at, and he wasn't there to take it out on. Damn him anyway for ruining a perfectly good steak dinner.

He smacked his hat down on the cheap motel bedside table and ran his fingers through his hair, trying to get himself back together before Dean got out of the bathroom. Jesus, he was. Something. Mad. Hurt. Sick of his family thinking he was still a kid after everything he'd been through.

He thought better of kicking the bed frame just about

the time Dean came out and scared him silly. "Shit!"

Dean blinked, jumped. "What? You forget I was here, Ace?"

"No. I was just thinking I had more time to sulk." He summoned up a grin, wanting to make sure Dean knew it wasn't him.

Dean shook his head, winked. "Now, now. You did notice you took up with an old-timer, right?"

"I may call you old man, but I more than have to work to keep up." Dean was **not** old enough to be his daddy. Damn it.

He got a long, quiet look. "You don't have to prove things to me, Ace. I know what we got."

His back went right down, the smile turning real. He just reached right out, taking Dean's hand. "I know. I just, well, ain't no lie to the whole thing about no one can get to you like family."

"You know it, Ace. That's why we don't hook up with kin. They'd drive us bug-nuts crazy." Those callused fingers squeezed his, rubbing a little.

"We still going to see your daddy?" Hell, now he was kinda scared to, supper with Roy having gone sour like it did. Not that Roy had been nasty or anything, but damn.

"You know it. He's not in good health and I want him to meet you, you know? Shake your hand and all." Dean smiled, the look a little bittersweet. "Want to know y'all saw each other."

Pulling Dean close, Will kissed the corner of Dean's mouth, just leaning a little, giving comfort. "I'd like that."

"Me, too." Dean's eyes caught his, all granite and sure. "Don't worry on your brother, Will. You and me? We're solid as stone."

Those eyes wouldn't lie. Will slid his arms around

Dean's waist, slipping his hands into Dean's back pockets. "We are. I'll not let it get to me."

"You gonna let me get to you instead?" Dean chuckled, winked at him. "Prove that I'm up to it?"

Oh, hell yeah. He arched his hips, rubbing belt buckles and other things all the way down. "Yeah. I think I am, cowboy."

"Oh, now. There's my Will..." Dean sorta pinked, lips snapping shut. Then Dean just pulled him closer, pulled him right in.

He didn't say anything, because what could he say? Wasn't like him to mope around, and he had been, and it had to suck for Dean. He just kissed Dean hard and deep, loving on him.

He got back twice what he gave. Dean hummed, moved against him, hips just rocking against him, sweet and steady.

Just humming, he moved against Dean, fingers curling around the hard muscles of Dean's ass and squeezing. How could there be anything wrong with what they had? There couldn't. Period. That settled in his mind, he was ready to get Dean in bed and show him, so he backed off and started working on the clothes.

"Mmm..." That sound was something else, low and deep, rich and just all about the want.

"Want you, cowboy. So bad." Dean put a need deep in his gut, made him want all sorts of things. He got Dean's shirt off, got that big belt buckle open, button and zipper, slipping his hand inside. "Want this."

"You got it. Lock, stock and barrel, Will." Dean's mustache tickled his jaw, his throat, that hot little tongue sliding on his skin.

"Barrel. Hell, yeah, cowboy." He squeezed, laughing, his chest free and loose finally. "I like it." God he loved this man.

"Good. I ain't going nowhere." Dean's lips found his earlobe, teasing it.

"Mmmhmm." Letting go wasn't high on his list, but he wanted to be naked, too, wanted to feel Dean against him, so Will let loose a minute, struggling out of shirt and belt and all.

Dean sat on the bed, thighs parted, eyes just watching him like he was a Sunday supper and needed eating up.

His boots went, thumping to the floor just as loud as his hat when he'd been slamming things around, but this time it was haste, not anger. Then his jeans. Then he was on the bed, hands sliding on Dean's skin, reaching around to trace the scars on Dean's back.

Dean's mouth was so hungry, running over his collarbone, the hollow of his throat, one nipple.

That made his skin tingle, made goosebumps rise up. He stroked and petted, legs rubbing Dean's, the hair catching. "Hot, cowboy. Very hot."

"Just wantin' a little of what you got, Will." The words were muttered against his skin, Dean's cock hard and hot against his thigh, making promises.

"Yeah. Love." He pushed between Dean's legs with his hips, rubbing and rubbing, lining their cocks up. Hot, damp. Fuck, yeah.

"Yeah." Dean's head snapped back, lips open, one hands landing on his ass. "Oh, fuck. That feels fine."

"Better than steak, for sure." Better than anything else had ever been or was likely to be. Dean was like fried chicken on Sunday after church, or like the perfect ninety point ride. He was home and adventure and hot, scarred skin that just made Will crazy.

"Better than fucking breathing, Will." He loved how Dean gasped, how Dean rocked and moved against him, shuddering when his fingers traced those ropy scars.

He just nodded against Dean's throat, breathing in

Old Spice and male musk, rocking and moaning. He reached down again, grasping both of them, tugging at their cocks. Just made him shake. One of Dean's legs draped over his, wrapping around and holding like he was trying to buck the man right off.

Bingo. Friction. Shoving against Dean, Will pressed, hips rolling. "Want. Please."

"Yeah. Yeah, gimme. Need it." Dean just met him head-on, hotter than a tin roof in August.

The kiss he took next curled his toes right up, made a shiver go up his spine, so good. Will's cock throbbed, and he moaned, so close. So close. Dean's hand joined his, thumb pressing into his slit, the dull burn making his hips buck.

"Fuck! Dean." His belly went hard as a board, and Will's back arched hard as he shot, his eyes just rolling, hands clutching.

"Fucking fine. So fucking fine, Will." Dean watched him, hips bucking, rubbing against their joined hands.

When he could see again he started stroking, started pulling again, needing Dean to be with him. "Come on, cowboy. Come on."

"Uh-huh. Uh-huh." Dean leaned right on into him, hips snapping, heavy cock burning against his hand. It didn't take long before Dean was shaking, coming for him, his name echoing in the room.

Oh, God, yeah. Will nuzzled Dean's chin, lips traveling up for a kiss, that mustache just tickling. "Damn, cowboy. What you do to me."

"Just love you." Dean took one soft kiss after another, tongue hot.

Lips swollen, Will kissed back, stroking Dean's sweaty back. "Same here, Dean. Love you. No matter what."

He grinned, shaking his head as he thought of Roy. Dean was his one big thing. And if his family didn't like it, well. They would after they got to know Dean. Nobody would be able to resist his cowboy for long.

Not even his stick in the mud brother.

Damn. Will hated fighting with his family. Hated it. And it wasn't like he was even fighting, though if he saw his brother again any time soon he was gonna sock him one on the jaw.

He'd called his mom for her birthday to see if she'd gotten her flowers and to ask for her green chile stew recipe, and what was she asking him about as soon as the please and thank yous were all done?

"I hear you've forgotten to tell me something, sweetie."

And of course, he was obstinate, deliberately misunderstanding. "I told you about Dean, mom."

"But honey, you didn't say he was that much older than you."

"That's because he's not."

"Roy says he is."

Will sighed, trying not to snap at her. Wasn't her fault. She hadn't met Dean, now had she? "Well, he wasn't looking close enough. I'm with him, Mom. Good or bad."

"Oh, honey. I just worry. I won't dwell on it anymore."

"Good."

They talked about the upcoming Deming craft fair and how his mom was going to try and sell some of those funny crocheted animals she made and about where he would be next week and yes, he would call. And all the while he could hear the suppressed concern in her voice.

Damn it.

"I love you, Mom."

"I love you too, honey. Be safe."

"I will."

Will hung up, and looked out of the little payphone kiosk to where Dean waited for him, scratching Sadie's ears. The look on Sadie's face was pure ecstasy. He had a feeling that's what he looked like when Dean petted him, too.

He grinned, shook his head. He probably hadn't heard the end of it from his folks, but Will didn't care. Dean was perfect.

Of course, maybe it was time to stop calling Dean old man.

Seven

Dean sat down hard on the bed, scowling to beat the band. He'd been thrown hard, railroaded and two stepped on. Bastard steer.

He'd managed to just talk Little George out of the hospital and into taking him to the hotel. He'd just left Will with the truck, the horses. He?

Needed a long soak and a few dozen drinks and a pain pill.

The knock at the door sorta interrupted that train of thought. "Dean? They didn't have another key. Let me in, cowboy."

"Aren't you due to ride again?" He levered himself up, hobbled to the door.

"I was. I dropped out. I've won my money tonight." Will had a bag of ice and a six-pack of beer. "Got the horses bedded down and came for you, cowboy."

"Oh, thank God for you." He almost whimpered. Almost. Will was so good to him.

"You took a beating. And you've done for me, Dean. Least I could do." Will grinned, leaned and kissed him.

He kissed right back, Will as welcome as showers in May. "I tell you what, Ace. I've been rode hard and put away wet."

"You have. Let's get those jeans off and get a look at that leg." Will tugged him back to the bed, undoing his belt and pushing down his jeans and sitting him down. "Oh, damn, Dean. That's gonna be Technicolor."

"Yeah, hurts like the dickens. Don't have the pennies for the doc though, you know, not for something that'll heal on its own."

"I know." Yeah. Will probably did know. Their finances weren't exactly solid. The hotel would take all of Will's winnings after they set aside enough for both of their entry fees for the next event. "Here, lemme ice that."

Fuck, but it was Hell getting old. Especially when the steers just got younger. "You want me to fetch a towel for it?"

"I'll get it. You sit tight. I'll start the tub filling while I'm in there. We'll have a bath so hot we can't hardly stand it."

"Oh, Hell yeah." He nodded and settled back, eyes closing against the pain. He could hear the familiar, good sounds of Will moving around, whistling, relaxed.

A soft touch came, Will pressing a towel-wrapped ice pack against the biggest of the bruises, easing the ache. Those hands massaged the knots, melting him a little.

He pulled Will down, took a long, slow lazy kiss. "You feel fine, Ace. Just fine."

"So do you, Dean. That bath ought to be ready." Will stood, smiled, the ice having been on longer than he thought what with them kissing and all.

He let his eyes drag down Will's bod, admiring the Hell out of his own personal cowboy. "You coming in, too?"

"You bet. I'm your cushion." Will winked, shucked clothes, steeping into the tub and turning the water off. "Come on, Dean. Let's float."

Dean nodded, let Will ease him down into the hot water and didn't worry on the weakness of that. They did for each other. "Oh. Oh, that's just right. Damn."

"Yeah. Oh, Dean, that's good." Will pulled him close, snugged his ass back against Will's lap. "You feel so good."

Fuck, but it felt decadent, leaning against Will, watching those hands on his body. He moaned from the sight alone, prick slowly filling, rising up like it needed Will's attention.

"Looks like something needs washing." Will laughed, nibbling his neck, hand coming down to close around his prick.

"Oh. You. You'd best watch that bit of rope, it tends to fly loose where you're concerned."

"You think?" That voice was just laughing in his ear, all relaxed and happy. He could feel Will's cock rising against his ass.

"I think. Hell, Ace. I might even know."

"Mmm." Will stroked him, fingers trailing from base to tip and back down. "I like that about you."

That touch made his toes curl. "Oh."

He leaned his head back, hands sliding down in the water to brush against Will's thighs. Will moved, rocking against him. Petting him. Kissing along his neck. He closed his eyes and just felt, Will building him up sweet and slow, the heat between them easy as pie.

Always gave him whatever he needed, his Will. Always just gave him everything. "Love. Hot."

Yeah. Will's hand was hot. Good. Tight around him.

"Mmmhmm. You set my world to right, Will." The combination of water and touch was enough to send him straight to Heaven.

"Good. You do wonders for mine." Sharp teeth threatened, Will pulling harder, that sweet, long cock prodding him.

He started rocking, moving, pushing up and up into that touch.

"Yeah. That feels good doesn't it? God, it's good to have the water." The water was perfect, easing his aches, giving them all of the buoyancy a tired body needed to get busy.

"Feels amazing. I needed this like nothing else."

"Mmmhmm." Slow and easy was turning fast and needy, he could hear it in the way Will's breathing changed, the way Will touched him, free hand moving over his belly, coming up to pinch his nipples.

"Oh... Damn..." He turned his face, mouth finding Will's jaw, Will's cheek.

Will leaned around, mouth meeting his in a scorching kiss that had his cock jerking and his sore muscles protesting. "Love you."

"Love. Damn. Will." He was panting with it, humping up into Will's hand.

"Oh. Gonna, cowboy. Gonna right now." Will squeezed him, pulled, and he could feel Will's prick jerking against his ass, heat sliding against him as Will came.

"Oh. Oh, that. So hot." He gasped, hand joining with Will's on his prick, squeezing his cock, bringing himself off.

"That's it. That's it, cowboy." Will helped him right over the edge, holding him so close, the water sloshing against the side of the tub.

He just relaxed, melted against Will with a moan. "Damn."

"Yeah. That took the rest of the starch right out. Love that." Will chuckled, petted him. "I figure a beer and some supper and we're in for the night."

"Sounds just about perfect." He leaned up, took a kiss. "You spoil this old man."

"It's mutual, yeah?" Easing him up, Will slid out from under him and stood, held out a hand to help him out of the slippery tub. "And it's my pleasure. Every damned day."

"Thank God for favors large and small, Ace." He hobbled back to the bed, let Will settle him. "Amen."

Eight

They jostled along the road. Christ, he needed to call Ron McMurtle to bring in a load of gravel. Daddy's old Ford would crack an axle, sure as shit.

The wind was blowing something fierce, the fields looking bare now, winter rye just beginning to come up. "That little frame house there? Belongs to Brenda Kaye. She runs the Brookshire's up in Greenville. Nice lady. Went to school with her boys. Me and Henry used to mow lawns in the summers when Daddy didn't need us."

They headed up the hill, the little grouping of bois d'arc standing there just like they'd always done. The farmhouse came into view right after, the place looking run down and tired, but as familiar as his own face in the mirror. Simple and square, painted robin's egg blue for Momma fifteen years ago and now more dove grey than anything -- it was home.

"Here we are."

Will looked around, eyes bright and curious. "Looks like a good place, ol... buddy. Got a nice big barn."

He chuckled, nodded. "There's the cattle barn and the horse barn, then there's one for hay and feed in the back a ways. You can't see the pond from here, either. Man, there used to be some nice bass fishing in there."

Miss Sadie's tail was going ninety to nothing, the old girl just panting. She'd been born here, had her own spot in the barn and Lord knew she loved Daddy half to death.

"Sadie looks like she knows." Grinning over, Will patted his leg. "So do you. Sometimes it's just good to be home, huh?"

"Yeah. I want to show you everything." He felt his cheeks heat, but it was true. This was... home. "Come on, let's go meet my daddy."

The screen door opened as he killed the engine, Daddy moving onto the porch. Something inside him twisted a little. Man. Man, Bubba'd said Daddy was getting on, but... Damn, no one'd said things were bad. Daddy'd lost a good thirty pounds, clothes just hanging on him, cheeks stubbled and drawn.

"Hey, old man! I'm home."

Will got out and went on around the truck, hanging back as he let Sadie out. Good deal, that, because Sadie broke the ice, limping right on up the steps to lick his daddy's hand.

"Well, well. Sadie-girl. You brought that gypsy-souled son of mine home for a minute." Daddy chuckled, smiled over. "Howdy, boy. You're a sight for sore eyes. This your Will?"

Dean nodded, smiled. Yeah. Yeah, it was. "Yes, sir. Will, this is my daddy, Joe Haverty. Daddy, Will Benton."

You could tell right off that Will was raised up right, because as soon as he was introduced he went on up and offered his hand. "Nice to meet you, Mr. Haverty."

"Call me Joe, son. Way Dean talks on you, you're family." Daddy shook Will's hand, then grinned wide.

"Come on in. The beer's cold and the First Baptist ladies brought King Ranch chicken over this morning."

The house was dark, dusty and Dean could see about a thousand things needed doing, but it could've been worse. "I'll warm it up in a minute, Daddy. Let's get some windows open, yeah? Then I'll put the horses in the barn. You got somebody coming to do feeding for you?"

His daddy wouldn't quite look at him as he nodded. "Sure. Sure I do."

Will just shifted from foot to foot a minute before padfooting to the kitchen and starting to fill the sink with water. There was a pile of dishes needing done, he could see.

He swallowed his sigh and got the windows opened. "So, how many head you running?"

He needed to make a list, hire someone to get out here once a day to check things. Hell, maybe if he leased out the back hundred for hay, that'd cover it. Looked like there was one window needed replacing and God knew what shape the barns were in. Fuck a duck.

"I... there was thirty head at the start of spring, son."

Lord. Start of spring?

Well, there could be forty-five or twelve left. Shit, Marthy.

"I'll have a ride tomorrow morning, if you want. Ride the fence, round everybody up and take a head count."

Laundry. Food. He needed to make sure there was money to buy feed for the winter and check the septic tank.

Change filters on the a/c.

Buy propane.

Drain the water heater.

Fuck.

By the time he'd made his mental list, Will was back,

wiping his hands on a dishtowel, smiling faintly.

"I put the chicken in the oven. There's clean plates and all. Mister... Joe. Sir. Would you like a beer? I bet Dean'd like one."

Oh, thank the good Lord for Will. He nodded, gave Will a real smile. "You know it, Ace. I'm plumb dry."

Daddy nodded. "I could use one. I... I'm sorry for the state of the place, son. It's been a long summer."

"Oh, now. Hey. We all get down in the bed sometimes. Won't take much to put it back to rights."

No, only the rest of this life and the next.

"We're off 'til the season starts back up, right, Dean?" The look Will gave him spoke all sorts of volumes, all about I know, and we can stay a bit and let me go get that beer. He came back a few minutes later, passing out open longnecks. "There now. We can sit a minute before we go unload the nags."

"How're they holding up? You still killing yourself on the broncs, boy? Or is the roping paying the bills?" Daddy settled back, asking all about the circuit, the critters, including Will right in. Daddy'd ridden back before Momma, knew the ropes and loved the sport. By the time the beers were finished, the casserole was smelling good and spicy and he was starting to feel less gobsmacked.

"You want to eat before we get the beasts or after, Ace?"

"Let's go ahead and get the critters." Will grinned over at his daddy, the look gentle as fuck. "You want to set the table, Joe? You've got clean dishes in there."

"Yeah? Yeah, I can do that. I'll make some tea, too." Daddy got himself up, moving toward the kitchen.

He watched for a second, fingers just ghosting over Will's wrist in thanks.

"I left the plates on the counter and the cups set up." Will took his hand, pressing his palm. "He should do. Do you want me to put up the horses? I can find my way, I'd bet, if you want to stay here."

"No. No, I need to..." Get outside for a minute. Catch his breath. Clear his head. "Check out the barns."

"All right. Come on then. We'll let him potter." Will led the way back out to the truck, just not saying much, letting him work up to it if he wanted to talk.

They got the horses moving, Sadie sleeping in the sun. The barn wasn't too bad, the stables relatively clean, the doors working. "Thanks for doing dishes, Ace. I appreciate it."

"No problem, Dean. No problem at all. You know, living alone you get a little careless with stuff like that. You should see my cousin Todd's house, and he's less than half your daddy's age."

Will stopped him just shy of going out the barn door, cupping his cheek in one hand and giving him a kiss. He leaned into it, one hand sliding around Will's waist. Oh. Oh, yeah. That made shit better.

"Mmm." That happy noise helped, too. Will just calmed him like nobody's business.

Just like gentling a horse. Lord. Still, it was something else and it felt so good, so damned right.

"You all right, cowboy?" Will stroked the back of his neck, fingers light and easy.

"Gonna be, yeah. I just... You know."

"Yep." He got another kiss, Will's lips warm and firm and good. They both smelled like horses and hay, and it felt like everything was normal, even when it was all screwed up. "Now, we ought to go rescue that fine smelling chicken before it burns up."

"Yeah, and make us a grocery list. I'd hate to starve." He found a real smile, a warm one.

"No shit. And your daddy? Has crap taste in beer." Oh, now Will had him laughing, the nut.

"You noticed that, did you? We'll need to get Ivory soap too -- he buys this brown shit that'll eat the varnish off a table."

"Well, I happen to like your skin on your body, cowboy."

Will looked like he'd just had a thought. "Am I gonna have to drag you down to the barn if I want to get frisky?"

"No way. Daddy knows that I, that we're an... us. I got a queen sized bed in my old room."

"Oh, good." Moving so close he could see each individual eyelash as Will blinked, Will kissed his throat. "Because I'm not willing to give that up."

"No. I'm not into lying and we're gonna be here a bit. You belong in my bed with me." The words tumbled out of him, all honest and raw.

Arms sliding about him to squeeze, Will nodded, hair brushing his ear. "Not my thing either, cowboy. Just you. You're my thing. We should go see about supper. And you need to spend some time, yeah?"

"Yeah. Yeah, I do. Come on. After I'll go get you an ice cream at the Dairy Queen." They headed back out into the twilight, into the house.

"Oh, now that sounds like heaven." Will just held on, hand slipping into his, comforting and squeezing. "A giant hot fudge sundae."

"Strawberry for me." He nodded, smiled as the door opened. Man, that chicken did smell good.

The barns were clean as a whistle, the windows and floors up at the house washed, and the one window replaced. Will had pulled almost six months worth of moldy stuff out of the fridge, and they'd cleaned out a lot more months worth of bad feed, but they were really getting a handle on it.

The work didn't bother him.

The haunted look in Dean's eyes did.

Dean was out in the barn, working on one of the tool handles with a roll of duct tape, when he went out with a travel mug of coffee.

"Hey, cowboy."

"Hey, Ace. How's it going?" Dean finished up the handle, hands working the duct tape tight, offering him a slow, tired smile. "Oh, is that coffee?"

"It is. Seemed a little too wet for lemonade or beer." It'd been drizzly all morning, and Will had laughed and laughed at how all three of them popped and cracked when they came to breakfast. Handing the coffee over, he moved right behind Dean, digging his fingers in to the muscles of Dean's shoulders. "Thought you needed some."

"I did. The damn weather just seeps right in my bones." Dean drank deep, tanned throat working, looking good against the light grey flannel.

Dean always looked good to him. Always. He bent and nibbled at Dean's neck. "Your daddy's napping in his chair."

"Mmm... is he? He can sleep pretty good..." Dean's voice got low and rough.

They just hadn't really had the energy to, well, yeah. They'd been working awfully hard. "Yep. Snoring away with Sadie on his feet."

"Even better. He'll hate to distract her." Dean walked him back into the shadows, one hand on his hip.

"Mmmhmm." Grinning, Will pressed right up against his cowboy, just jonesing on being able to rub a little, kiss a little.

Dean leaned back against the wall, rocking them

together, the heat building right on up. The smell of wood and hay and horse and Dean all together was just right.

Yeah. Hell, yeah. He kissed Dean nice and deep, pushing his tongue in rhythmically. He gripped Dean's hips, pushing in good and tight, giving them both some friction. He felt the 'oh', the ripple that moved through his cowboy, letting him know that yeah, right there. Damn.

Hoo boy. He was gonna pop, they weren't careful. It had been just long enough... "Dean. I. Oh."

"Gonna let me..." Dean's voice trailed off as that lean body just slid down the wall, fingers working his jeans open. "Want."

"Oh. Oh, Dean." He was torn between just standing there and watching and dropping to his knees, too, so he could touch and feel. He wavered just long enough to feel Dean's mustache on his skin, and then his brain shorted out and decision making was beyond him.

Dean's mouth was like pure fire on him, hands wrapped around his thighs damn near as hot. He was gonna fly with it, heat and need flooding him right off.

Every muscle in his body tensed up, his belly tight, thighs jumping. He knocked Dean's hat off trying to find a solid hold on something. Finally he got a grip on Dean's shoulders, his hips rolling.

Dean didn't hold anything back, pulled him in deeper and deeper, sucking hard. He didn't hold back either, just really getting a rhythm with his hips. He loved how Dean loved him. He surely did.

Those strong fingers tightened, tugged him right on in, throat closing on the tip of his cock, squeezing it, making his eyes roll.

Boom. That was it. Will cried out, coming so hard he shorted out for a minute, his ears ringing. Dean nuzzled his lower belly, mustache tickling, making his skin tingle.

"Damn." His knees hit the hard-packed floor of the

barn, and he pulled Dean close for a kiss, tasting himself there. He worried the zipper on Dean's jeans, wanting to return the favor any way he could.

So hard. So hot -- Dean's cock was pushing at those jeans, trying to leap right into his hand.

Took him forever, but he got that stubborn zip open, closing his hand around Dean's sweet cock, stroking clumsily. So good. Had anything in his life ever felt so good. "Cowboy. Love."

"Uh-huh. Just like that, Will. Just like that." Dean looked stunned, dazed, lips parted as he moaned.

"Yeah. You look. Oh." Dean looked good, not so tired, not so old. It made him feel huge.

Dean nodded, lips pushing against his. Those hips were jerking and snapping, driving that sweet shaft into his hand.

Will gave that kiss up, let Dean take it where he wanted to go. He stroked and petted, his other hand on Dean's back, sliding down Dean's spine. He could feel Dean's need in the way that tongue fucked his lips, the way those hips jerked and spread wet heat over his palm.

"Mmm. Yeah. Oh, Dean. Needed that." They'd just been so tired and tense and... poor Dean. It had to be hard. Will knew he never had to worry on it like Dean did. Roy would take care of mom and dad.

"Uh-huh. Uh-huh, needed you." Dean smiled, nuzzled his jaw a little. "More than coffee, even."

The coffee mug lay on the ground a few feet away, and Will just chuckled. "Good thing it's aluminum. Tell you what. You can have more coffee later, along with the dump cake I made."

"Works for me, Ace. Daddy might just try to kidnap you and keep you forever."

"Well, that depends on how he feels about canned cherry pie filling." Will laughed, then groaned as he heaved up off the floor and his leg twinged. He pulled Dean up, too. "Besides. I belong to you, lock, stock and soul."

"That's right and I aim to keep you." Dean's hand stroked his thigh a second. "Long hot bath for you tonight, mister."

"For both of us. We'll put Joe to bed and soak." That sounded like heaven. Right there on earth with Dean. That was even worth cleaning the bathroom for.

Which if they were gonna soak? Was next on his list.

Eight

The little one foot pre-decorated tree twinkled in the corner. The tiny cabin kitchenette bubbled and baked with the fine scents of beef roast and pecan pie. "Please Come Home for Christmas" played on the radio, and Will wouldn't want to be anywhere but where he was, holding Dean tight, swaying along with the music.

They'd decided to get a little rented cabin and spend it together, just the two of them. He was happy as a tick on a hound.

Will nuzzled Dean's temple, kissing lightly. "This is good."

Dean was stretched out, wearing a pair of bright red socks and the oldest pair of jeans on earth, looking relaxed and lazy and fine as frog hair. "Hell, yeah, Ace. You had a damned fine idea here."

"I love my folks. But damned if I could see spending another Christmas explaining myself. Over and over." He grinned, brushing his lips against Dean's, the tiny rub of that moustache sending tingles down to his toes.

Dean chuckled, one hand warm on his belly, eyes crinkling up. "You see, Momma -- that old cowpoke? I sold my soul to him for a t-bone and I can't reckon a way out of keeping him."

He laughed out loud, rolling to cover Dean with his body. "Damned straight, cowboy. But you know moms. They want grandbabies."

"Yeah. Well, I don't see that happening here, do you? How does your mom feel about puppies?" Dean's hand slid down his spine to cup his ass.

"Mmm. She, uh, makes them sleep in the barn." Damn it was hard to think with Dean's hands on him. That was the very best part about a not family Christmas. The touching, unselfconscious and real.

"Mmm... 's a nice ass... I mean, barn." Dean's eyes had gone all warm and wanting, sun-dried silk lips brushing along his neck.

"Yeah?" Will shifted, letting his legs fall to either side of Dean's and pressing down against the warm bulge hardly hidden by Dean's thin jeans.

"Uh-huh..." Those hands tightened, pulling him down harder, Dean rubbing against him. "Feels fine, Ace. Damned fine."

"Does, doesn't it? We got plenty of time before dinner." He kissed Dean hard, tongue pushing in, so hungry suddenly, so needy.

Dean opened right up, a low, rich moan that was sweeter then Tupelo honey vibrating his lips. He could taste coffee and cream and a hint of peppermint. Oh, somebody'd been sneaking candy canes.

Will went searching for every bit of mint he could find, letting the kiss go on until they just had to breathe. "Oh. Dean."

Dean's breath was coming fast, that pink tongue sneaking out to lick at their lips. "Yeah, Will. Want."

Not one for flowerdy speeches, his cowboy.

That was damned fine with him. That way he didn't have to think up something to say that would match. All

Will had to do was kiss, and push back to work at Dean's jeans, wanting more skin. In response, Dean pushed his flannel off, then started tugging his t-shirt out of his waistband.

As soon as he got Dean's pants down, Will helped, stripping off, not bothering to take time to tease. He never was one for unwrapping his gifts slowly. Damned if that wasn't a feast of skin he couldn't wait to dive into, and Will went for one pink nipple, licking and sucking.

"Oh..." Dean arched up into him, hips rubbing up against him.

"Yeah." Moving on to the other, Will rubbed his stubbly cheek against it, feeling the bit of skin rise against him. "Taste good, cowboy."

"Your mouth is something else. Feel you down in my belly." Dean pushed callused hands into his waistband, fingers hot on his ass.

He wiggled, giving Dean more of his skin. "Yeah? Where else do you want to feel it?"

"Is there anywhere I don't want it?" Dean chuckled, pinching his ass nice and firm.

He chuckled, rubbing good and hard in return. "Well, then, I'd better get busy."

Starting with Dean's throat, Will licked and kissed and nipped his way down to Dean's belly, nuzzling into the warm skin there, getting a good dose of Dean's scent.

The skin there was just barely tanned, a sprinkling of salt and pepper hair leading him down a pleasure trail.

He teased that little trail of hair with his chin, then his lips, heading right down to plant a kiss on the tip of Dean's cock. "Oh, yeah. Could put my mouth right there for you."

"I reckon I could... Oh... Could live with that decision, Will."

"You think? 'Cause I wouldn't want to put you out."

Will hid a grin by bending to mouth Dean's balls.

Dean snorted, legs parting, tight little ass sliding on the sheets.

Oh, damn. Now he could think of another place he wanted to put his mouth. He lifted that hot, muscled little butt in his hands, moving gently so as not to strain Dean's back, and spread those lean thighs, pushing between to lick Dean's hole.

"Will..." Oh, now, was there anything finer than the sound of his name, called out like that? All low and rough and raw?

Nothing in the whole wide world. Will kept at it, loving and licking and panting for breath. God, he loved Dean's tight cowboy bubble of a butt.

Dean planted his feet, spread wide and wanting, moving into his hands, his mouth, low cries filling the air.

So damned pretty. So good. The taste was wild, dark, and Will just went for it, getting Dean so wet, opening him so wide. Then he wet his fingers and pushed two in, lowering Dean's hips enough to suck that sweet cock, taking it in deep.

"Sweet Lord!" Dean's shoulders left the mattress, ass grinding down onto his fingers. "Will!"

"Mmmhmm." He worked Dean, fingers pushing in and out, mouth going up and down. The flavor and scent of Dean meant home, no matter where they were, and Will soaked it up greedily.

Dean rode him hard, bucking for him, cock sliding deep as Dean moaned, wicked promises filling the air.

He'd hold the man to those promises. Every one of them. For now he would just try to find the lube and nail Dean to the mattress. He pulled off and out, holding Dean down with one hand and searching with the other. There. Yeah. Will got himself all slicked up, and Dean too, and slid in, opening Dean right up.

Christ, those eyes were wild, desperate, Dean's hands hard on his hips and pulling him deeper. "God, yes. Will. Love."

"Yeah. Yeah, Dean." Will pumped his hips, pushing in, tracing Dean's face with his hand. "Love you."

Dean's mustache tickled his palm, then the heat of that soft tongue stroked his skin. Oh. Oh, he couldn't hold it much longer. His hips snapped, losing the rhythm, just pounding Dean.

Two of his fingers were pulled into that hot mouth, sucked hard as Dean grunted, ass clenching tight around him, heat spraying between them. Will groaned low, filling Dean deep and hard, his own heat pumping out of him, biting down on one of Dean's fingers.

Dean was breathing hard, low moans sounding. "Damn. Damn, Will. You feel good."

"Mmm." Will slumped, coming down to cuddle up with Dean, stroking damp skin with his fingers. "Always, cowboy."

Dean's lips brushed his temple. "I'm liking this type of Christmas, I'm thinking."

Grinning, Will kissed Dean hard, nodding before sniffing to make sure nothing was burning. All he could smell was him and Dean. Damn it was good.

"Yeah. I could spend every Christmas this way, cowboy."

"You've got yourself a deal." Dean patted his ass, then tugged the blanket over them.

"Good."

Yeah. Dean felt like home. And there was nothing like being home for Christmas. Nothing like it at all.

Nine

Dean'd left Will back at the campground when he went hunting for a phone, not because he didn't want Will to hear, but because...

Well, some shit a young man didn't have to hear about, and him and Allen having a bit of a go-round? Was one of 'em.

He dialed the private number in Allen's office, sighing as his brother answered. "Haverty here."

"Allen, 's me."

"Dean? I didn't expect to hear from you so soon. How's things?" He plumb hated that sound in that voice, all skittish and cool, waiting for some damn bad news. Hated worse that he had some.

"Me and Will just spent a few days up at the farm, Bubba. Daddy ain't doing so good. He's needing."

"Well, then. You know what I think on that. We need to sell the land, Dean."

He shook his head, looking up at the trees, feeling the urge to slam the phone down. "That land's been in our family for five generations. We got kin buried on the land."

"That land's worth enough money to put Daddy in a good home for a good, long time and still have enough left over to maybe live on after you run yourself ragged."

"Oh, fuck that. Daddy don't need some minimum wage fucking nurses wiping his ass. It'd kill him." His daddy was a good man, a strong man. One hell of a cowboy, Dean'd not have him go to strangers.

"Dean, man, he's *dying* and I've seen the bills coming in. He's been missing tax payments; he's going to lose the damned land."

"What?" The news shook him, hurt him deep and he couldn't help the growl. "Goddamnit, Allen! What the fuck have y'all done?"

"Me? You're the one saying Daddy's okay, doesn't need a home."

"He doesn't need a home, you little prick! He needs a family!"

Allen snorted. "I have a family, Dean. Three kids, a house, a wife, a career. What the fuck do you have? A sweet little blond fuckbuddy and a five year old pickup."

"How much?"

Dean listened to the silence for a minute, listened to the sound of his heart pounding, then Allen spoke. "How much what?"

"How much does he owe?"

"Right at eight thousand dollars."

Christ. Sweet Christ. His knees buckled a little, but he kept his voice calm. "I'll pay the taxes."

"It's just land, Dean."

"Not to me. Not to me. That's... that's home, Bubba. I'll pay the taxes."

He heard Allen sigh. "Fine. It's your home, your land. Go home and take care of it."

"No. It's **Daddy's** land. It's Haverty land. It's..."

"Whatever. I don't think it's that important."

"I gotta go. I got plans to make."

He didn't wait for Allen's goodbye. He just hung up

the phone and headed back to camp.

Plans to make. Bulls to ride.

He was scared.

Not worried. Not nervous.

Scared.

He hadn't sat on a bull since the accident, and he'd been younger then. Stronger. Practiced.

He'd had nothing to lose but his entry fees.

Now he had Daddy's land. His family's place. Will.

Christ. He shook his head, looking over at a tight face, Will's lips pursed, angry. Bad enough to hear he was fixin' to go home in three months, but to hear he was going to push for the tax money?

Hell, he might just've lost himself Will before he ever killed himself on that big bastard in the chute.

The few times he'd tried bull riding, back in his lean and desperate days, using a friend's rigging and holding on for dear life, Will had decided it wasn't for him.

For one thing, he was too damned tall. Horses had longer legs, so bronc riding was all right, but if they put him on a stubby bull, he couldn't get his feet hooked right. Will'd ridden two bulls out of a total of twelve, the rest of them piling him off hard enough to break ribs and sprain knees, one of them spilling him hard enough to scatter his chickens but good, leaving him with a concussion and a broken thumb.

That one was the last one, and the one that convinced Will that bullriders had a screw loose, much as he admired them, and as much as he wished he could be where the money was.

So naturally, Dean having been a bullrider by trade, that was what Dean went to when he needed money, bad back and all. Made Will crazy, but he knew better than to complain. A man had his pride, and his need for home.

So he just sat in the stands and bit his damned fingernails and prayed for Dean to come off those bulls in one piece.

Because he didn't know what he'd do without the man.

Not one bit.

Ten

Dean'd been restless. Edgy as a cat in a roomful of rocking chairs. Ever since he'd won that big purse, he'd been less **there**. More somewhere Will couldn't go.

He pushed the last of his green chile enchiladas around the plate, sopping up the refried beans. They'd ordered sopapillas, and he figured it was as good a time as any to ask while they waited.

"So what's the bee in your bonnet, cowboy?"

Dean looked up, eyes just as dull and unhappy as they could be. "I... I got a call from Troy Martin, the minister up at Emory. He'd heard I'd sent that money in for the taxes on Daddy's land."

Dread settled in his gut. "Yeah? He gonna look in on the old man every so often?"

"No. I mean, probably, but that ain't what he wanted." Dean sighed, fork playing with the carne guisada he hadn't eaten, face just as grey as winter skies. "The man says Daddy needs someone full time, that if someone doesn't come to stay, the county'll get involved."

The hair rose up on the back of his neck. "I don't suppose Allen will hire anyone in." He didn't mean to say anything against Dean's brother. The man surely had his reasons. Surely. But it was a hard thing, to see Dean deal with all of it.

"Allen wants me to put him in a home, Ace. I won't do that." Dean looked at him, straight and sure. "I have to go to home and take care of him, Will. I have to."

Will blinked. Set his fork aside very carefully and just blinked. Somehow he'd known... He took a deep breath.

"'Course you do. Ain't no one else gonna do it."

"No. No, there ain't." Dean sighed, rubbed the back of his neck. "I been thinking on things and, well, if you'll bring me and Miss Sadie and Blueboy on home, I'll let you take the truck and trailer. I mean, Gypsy needs somewhere to sleep and all."

"You. I mean. You'd let me take Gypsy?" That was. Well, that was just like his cowboy. "I can send some on home to you, to help out. Gypsy and I been winning some."

"Well, I want you to keep you in proper working order, but..." Dean sighed again, eyes on the table. "It ain't your trouble, you know? I mean, I won't think less of you if you don't. I just... This ain't how it's 'sposed to be."

"How's anything supposed to be anything but what it is?" Hell, his heart was just racing, and he wanted to scream, but Dean didn't need that. He needed Will to be strong. "We'll ride tomorrow, since Sunday is the big purse day. Then we'll take you home. And it's my trouble if it's yours, Dean." He just reached out, covered Dean's hand with his. That was all there was to it.

Dean nodded, squeezed his fingers. "Gonna miss the Hell out of you, Ace."

"Yeah. I. Well, I'd stay with you, Dean. But I got some good riding yet." The sopapillas came, the waiter kinda giving them a look, but Will ignored it.

"Yeah. I know." Dean handed him over the honey,

gave him a bare smile. "I know."

They ate dessert in silence. There wasn't much else to say.

But even the whole bottle of honey wasn't gonna make it taste better.

It was a shit drive from Edinburg to Emory and Will had to get back to Brownsville right quick, so there wasn't gonna be any long drawn-out goodbyes. Hell, they'd pulled up about three in the morning and crashed for a bit, now it was noon and Will was needing to go again.

He hopped up into the trailer to get Blueboy. God knew he'd need one horse to ride fence and the old bastard wasn't ever gonna be what Will needed. Gypsy though? She was a good'un and thought Will just hung the moon or held the ladder for the fella that did.

Dean gave Gypsy some love before taking Blueboy out. "You be good to him. Make him some decent money and no colicking."

"She's a good girl. She'll miss Blue and Sadie." Will came around, hands in his pockets, legs up to there.

He nodded. "Yeah. I got my stuff from the back, but I got some papers for you."

He kept all his important papers in a little metal box with a lock. There was a spare in the garage, no surprise there, Daddy used to keep bullets in one, so he reckoned Will could have his box. It had a bill of sale for Gypsy, for the Chevy and the trailer. It had Gypsy's vet records, his emergency information, a copy of his will.

"Okay." Will just kinda blinked at him. His blue-eyed boy'd been doing that a lot lately. Not that he could blame him. This had all been... fast.

He went to the truck, unlocked the box again. "Here's

the truck papers. Here's Gypsy's stuff. Here's all the bills of sale. This is all my information, if you need it."

"Dean. You don't have to." Just stunned, that's what Will looked like. "I just. Well. Damn."

He couldn't help but smile. Like he'd leave one of his own without the things he needed.

Will just came over, helping him get Blue settled in the barn, working right along. Then Will came to him, looping those long arms around his waist, leaving them cheek-to-cheek.

"I got to go."

"Yeah. Make sure you get some good breakfast at El Pato's, okay?" He closed his eyes, just breathed in deep, just in case this was...

Well, just in case.

"I will. As soon as I get some money saved up I'll get a cell phone. Until then I'll just have to call from the hotels or camps. You need me, you call the arena. You've got my schedule."

"I do. You need me, you call." He wasn't going anywhere.

Kissing his cheek, the corner of his mouth, Will nodded. "I'll call. You count on it. Need my dose of you." Will sighed, pulled back enough to look him in the eye. "I'll be around, you know?"

His chest hurt, deep and dull and he thought he'd never get a full breath again. "I know. You be careful with you."

"And you don't work yourself into the ground." He got a kiss, one that lingered just long enough for him to taste all the words Will didn't say.

He couldn't swallow over the shit that was stuck in his throat, so he just walked Will to the truck, made sure there was oil and coolant and the Mapsco all tucked in the floorboard in the back. The cooler had cokes and ice and a six-pack for later. Will was good to go.

Will nodded, kissed him again, this time deep and hard enough to bruise, before turning back to the truck and opening the door. Grabbing his hat from the seat, Will put it on, hiding his eyes.

"I'll see you maybe next month, cowboy. On my way back through."

"I'll be here. You tell the boys hi for your old man." He looked at his keychain, swinging from the ignition and had to fight, really and truly fight the urge to get in the truck and go. Just drive and drive.

"I will. You take care."

Then his chance to just leave passed him by, because Will'd turned the engine over and pulled out, one hand poking out the window to wave goodbye, leaving him nothing but the dust the truck kicked up.

He watched until he couldn't see the truck anymore, just standing in the driveway like a kid waiting for the school bus.

"Love you, Will, more than damn near anything."

Then he went to fix Daddy's lunch and get to work. Damned roof needed mending and he needed to see if he couldn't get that Ford running again.

Eleven

His days were different now and he fought the urge to growl, to sit in the bed long after the critters needed feeding, to sit at the table late at night and watch the fuzz on channel 39 and drink another beer and another.

Dean didn't resent Daddy being sick and old and needing. He didn't. He worked hard -- got Daddy up and into his chair, cleaned up, fed, shaved. Once a week they went into Greenville to see the doctor and to spend a day in occupational therapy which Dean figured was a fancy-assed term for old guy day care so he could hit Wally World and the feed store and the lumber yard because damn, the house needed work.

And he knew he was doing the right thing. Knew he was being a good man. Hell, that's why he'd ridden the bulls so hard the last go round, so he'd have the money to help Daddy out. And Allen was right -- there was a big difference between a big-city Houston lawyer making big money and a broke-dick cowboy with a pickup and a long-toothed horse making thirty-grand a year.

Still.

Sometimes he'd catch the standings in the paper or on the late-news and he'd know that Will was out there living and he was sitting in this falling-down house with Daddy fading every day and it would make him shake with wanting to hit something.

Those were straight-up whiskey nights, yessir.

God, he was dead tired. His back was killing him, he'd been stepped on when he got bucked off last night, and his head throbbed from staring into the sun all afternoon.

Will was ready to be home. The first few months back on the circuit without Dean had been hard. The first finals rodeo even harder, even though Dean made a point at being at the one big purse event Will managed to make.

But two weeks into the second season? Will was feeling Dean's absence like a separate ache, worse than his back or his head. He was finding reasons not to work the Kansas circuit anymore, or the New Mexico-Colorado route, staying close to Texas and Dean and making those trips home every three or four weeks.

He had some hard thinking to do.

With Dean's little spread in sight, though, and the thought of Dean's skin under his hands taking up his whole brain? Anything else would have to wait.

Dean tugged off his work boots, left them in the mudroom with a thud. Fucking gumbo damn near sucked the calves hip deep and, lord, wasn't he tired?

He started himself a pot of coffee and went in to check on Daddy. He closed the bedroom window against the rain and turned down the light, chuckling at the freight train snoring that he'd lived with his whole life.

Lord, lord.

A bacon sandwich, a cup of coffee and a Twinkie and he was set -- his little TV on, cigarette waiting for after dinner. Life was...

Well, vaguely shitty, honestly.

Dean chuckled at himself, reached for the phone. He reckoned he knew how to make it better.

The phone rang three times before he got a sleepy, "'Lo?"

Oh, shit. "I didn't mean to wake you, Ace. I'll let you go."

"Huh? No!" He could hear shifting and clicking, covers sliding. "Hey, cowboy. Man, it's good to hear your voice. I was just dozing to the TV."

"Watching anything good?" He grinned, settling the phone on his shoulder. "There's nothing but crap on here."

"I don't even know what... oh. It's just CMT. So how's it going, cowboy?" Warm and really sounding happy to hear him, just like he'd said, Will's voice eased him some.

"Weather's for shit, but I guess I can't complain. Got a couple momma cows fixin' to calve any second. Daddy's snoring. Same old, same old."

"Some things don't change. So, I got to tell you, I saw old Jack Lawson today. He asked after you. Got me to missing you fierce."

"Yeah?" He shifted, smiled. He knew all about missing. "Miss Gypsy treating you right? Your leg being good?"

"Miss Gypsy is a doll, but my leg can kiss my ass. It's been shitty." The phone clunked and Will grunted. "Sorry, getting comfy. How's your daddy?"

"Old. Crotchety. Smells like cheese." One of his eyebrows raised. "How comfy?"

"Well. I'm not wearing nothin' but an ice pack." He

could hear the laughter, but he could hear a hint of husk creeping into Will's voice, too.

"Oh, ho!" He chuckled, shifted a little at the thought that brought up. "Ace, man. That ice pack? Belongs on your knee."

"These days it belongs somewhere else. Did I mention missing you, cowboy?"

He cleared his throat, nodding. "Yeah. Yeah, once or twice. Feels like it's been a month of Sundays since we... you know."

"Yeah. Yeah it does." Will sounded just as, well, needy as he did, voice low and harsh. "I want you, Dean. Want to be there with you, touching you."

"Oh..." His toes just curled right up, cock jumping. "Oh, hell yes. My bed's so fucking empty without you in it."

In it, naked and spread, those legs going and going and going...

Damn.

"Same way here." He could hear Will breathing, hear each inhalation, faster than the last. "I keep thinking. And I. Well, I tell you, it's lonesome. Some nights I hurt."

Lord, that boy had a mouth on him. The things he said.

"There's things I want, Will. So bad. Wake up in the nights, hard for you." He felt his cheeks going hot, but it was just the truth. His hand dropped down, rubbing through the denim of his jeans.

"Yeah. God, Dean. Want my mouth on you. Want to taste you. Want you in me."

"Oh. Oh, yeah." He damn near whimpered, balls drawing up. "Want to touch you, feel you in my hand."

"Oh, Dean, your hands. Rough skin and sweet touch. Yeah." Something thudded lightly on the other end. He'd bet the icepack had gone the way of the dodo.

He was fucking burning up, cock pushing against his zipper. "Love the sounds you make, the way you look against me."

"And I love your scars and your skin and your mustache on me." Will gave him a deep moan. "Damn, Dean."

"Will..." He couldn't bear it, he had to unzip, touch. Oh. Oh, yeah.

"Are you? I am. I just can't help it, cowboy. Need to."

"Yeah. Yeah, I just... Fuck, wish it was you." He slid down in the easy chair some, hips pushing up.

"I know." That sweet-honey voice went lower. "I do, too. God, I wish I was there."

"Mmmhmm... On the bed all spread out..." He groaned, eyes closing as he imagined his tongue sliding up those long, long thighs.

"You looking at me, touching me. Yeah. I'm all for that. All about it. Next time I see you, I swear to God I'll be ready before I ever get to you, just gonna ride you."

"Oh. Oh, shit. Yeah. Yeah, Will. Love that, watching you." He arched, feet pushing into the floor, helping his hips up into his touch.

"Uh-huh. Uhn. So hard for you." The phone creaked, and he knew. He knew what Will was doing.

Oh. Oh, fuck. "Yeah. Yeah, Will."

His thumb dragged over the tip of his cock, his eyes just rolling.

"Dean!" It was a cry, ringing in his ear, and he could hear Will just moaning, panting, breath finally starting to slow. "Come for me, cowboy. Please."

He whispered Will's name as he shot, the sound all about promises and needs and yeah. Yeah.

"Mmm." Will just purred for him, so good; with his eyes closed he could believe Will was there. Just for a minute. "I was thinking. Maybe I could swing through this week."

"You think?" He smiled, nodded. "I'd sure like that, Will. We could have ourselves a visit."

"We could. I could stay a bit, let my knee heal up, let Gypsy sit with Blue and Sadie a bit."

"Oh, that sounds good. I'll get some icy hot, some brisket." He was too old to get this excited, but damn he was ready to visit a day or three.

"I'll be there by Tuesday." There was something. A catch in Will's voice. Told him he wasn't alone. Not one bit.

"I'll be waiting. You take care of that leg, now." He grabbed some tissues, cleaned himself up. "Glad I woke you up."

"I am, too. Cowboy. I am, too. You get some sleep and say hey to your daddy."

"I will. See you Tuesday, Ace." He smiled as he hung up, grabbed the little pad of paper and started making himself a grocery list. Will was coming home to visit.

Wooboy.

He'd hit rain in El Paso. He'd run out of gas in some tiny town outside of Abilene, and had to wait until Monday morning for the gas station/grocery/Post Office to open so he could get the truck filled up. The flat tire in Fort Worth told him he probably ought to be learning a lesson from all this, but Will just kept humping his load until he got his ass back to Dean.

Gypsy knew where they were. He could tell by the way she practically killed him getting out of the trailer, by the way she went looking for old Blueboy in the barn. Will shook his head, grinning at the silly beasts. Hell, he couldn't bitch. He felt the same way. He was wanting some iced tea and some cobbler and just to see those greeny gray eyes smiling at him.

He went on up to the house after feeding and rubbing Gypsy down, knocking on the door and standing outside with his hat in his hands.

"Who is that I hear at my door?" That drawl was just... Man. Someone was happy to see him.

"A tired, stinky rider looking for his very own cowboy?" Will just grinned so wide his cheeks hurt, looking Dean over carefully.

The man looked drawn. Sort of faded, maybe. Happy, though. Real happy. "Come in, then, and sit a spell."

"Glad to." Will went right on in, putting his hat aside, looking ruefully at his boots. "You want me to take these off? They're pretty done in."

"You'd best; we'll get them resoled in town." Dean took his bag from him, and then stole a quick kiss. "Oh, I been needing that. You want a beer?"

"Yeah. After you give me one more of those." He needed the kisses more than the beer.

That got him a smile, slow and sweet as honey over good biscuits. "I can handle that, Ace. More than handle it."

Then he got eased back against one of those old wallpapered walls, Dean's mustache tickling his lips, tongue pressing right in. Oh. Oh, yeah. God, that felt like home, even if the house looked alien and his boots were still covered in muck. Will just wrapped his arms around Dean's waist and kissed hard, tasting lemonade and salt.

Dean's hand cupped his cheek, tilting his head down and drawing him right on in. He could feel Dean wanting, the bulge hot against his thigh.

His own cock rose up high and hard, just needing so bad. It had just been too damned long. Dean smelled good, felt good, and Will went with it, rocking against Dean, soaking him in.

"Bedroom. Will. Please." Dean groaned, teeth scraping on his lips.

"We won't disturb him, will we?" Dean's daddy was his family, and there was no way he wanted to disrupt the man's sleep. He'd go to the barn first.

"No. He's on the far side and the springs don't creak bad."

Oh, there was some hunger in that voice.

"Bed then." Taking Dean's hand he scooted out, pulling him along. He was just needing fierce. "Missed you so, cowboy."

"You know it. Been the longest few months in history." The bedroom had been painted since he was there last, a picture of him riding Miss Gypsy in a frame on the bedside table.

Oh. He grinned, feeling silly and proud all at once. He had a little folding frame of Dean at their last event together that he put out wherever he stayed, camp or hotel. He pounced as soon as the door closed behind them, kissing hard.

Dean wrapped those strong hands around him, one around his nape, one at his waist, tugging them together. He loved how Dean opened up, let him in deep.

Sometimes he figured he must be crazy as hell to leave this every time he came back here. Will struggled with Dean's shirt, thanking the good lord above that it was oldfashioned snaps, not buttons.

He got little grunts and moans, his t-shirt tugged out of his jeans. Pulling it off over his head wasted precious seconds, but he did it, and then it was his skin against Dean's. His own moan sounded loud and shocking.

"Oh, sweet Jesus." Dean got them moving toward the bed, hands shaking a little as they worked his buckle.

"Need."

"Yeah. Oh, Dean. Yeah." He wanted so bad. They shucked the rest of the clothes, and before he even knew it they were on the bed together, sliding on the old quilt.

Dean tugged him up along him, one leg wrapping around him, pulling them good and close. Will settled in, rubbing, his cock sliding along Dean's thigh. He was wet at the tip, so hot he figured he was just gonna explode.

"Can smell you. Will. Damn." Dean bucked, cock jerking, leaving wet kisses on his skin.

"Yeah. Yeah. Us together. Love." Bending, he kissed Dean deep, finally getting them lined up and their cocks sliding along each other.

Dean grunted, hand on his ass, rocking them, moving them good and hard, taking them for a ride.

His eyes tried to shut, but he forced them to stay open so he could see, so he could watch Dean. "Oh, cowboy."

He rode hard, just held on as Dean bucked.

"Yeah." Dean's eyes just ate him up, cheeks flushed dark, heat spreading over his belly.

"Oh. Fuck, Dean!" That was it. Every muscle in his body clenched, and he shot so hard he couldn't breathe to cry out. God, he'd missed this man.

"Oh, good to see you. So good." Dean gasped, groaned as they relaxed. "How was your drive?"

"Rotten." Chuckling, he told Dean about the big old lady who had changed his tire on the side of the road after he'd refused a ride in her big rig. "But it was worth it to get here."

Dean chuckled, hands constantly moving, rubbing his back, working out all sorts of sore.

"Mmm." Damn, that made him all but purr. "How're you doing, cowboy? How's your daddy?"

"He's going downhill, but he's comfortable. I think he's glad I'm here, fixing stuff. This old house was in sad,

sad shape."

"Whatever eases him. It's good, you having something to do, too." He knew Dean well enough to know his cowboy hated being idle, hated having too much time to dwell on things. "Anything you need me to help with while I'm here, you holler."

"Mmm... I have a serious case of blue balls with your name all over it." He got a grin, a wink, a quick, hard hug.

"Oh, hell yeah." That he could help with. "I bet I stink to high heaven. But if you can stand me, I'll just stay here and see what I can do about it."

"You don't stink, Ace. You smell like home."

God. He hugged Dean tight, nuzzling into that brown-skinned throat. "You feel like home. I tell you, cowboy, it's been a rough month or two."

"Yeah, I hear that. Wanna hear all that's gone on. Every bit." Dean's hand smoothed his hair, the sound of that steady heartbeat just fine.

"I got about a week. I'll tell you all of it, I promise. Right now I just want. Well. I want you, Dean. Want to just be." Wanted to touch, to taste, or hell, just to cuddle.

"You got it. Me. Whatever." Dean grinned, chuckled sweet and low.

"Good." He was tired as all get out, feeling lazy in his bones, but he couldn't stop touching. He kissed Dean's chin, stroked his breastbone, listened to the thump thump of Dean's heart.

"Mmm..." Dean hummed some, hands all about loving him, warm and strong and just right.

"You know it. This is just what the doctor ordered." He had a sudden image of Gypsy and Blue snuggling up out in the barn and chuckled.

"What's funny, Ace?" Dean leaned, nuzzled his

temple. "God, you're looking good."

"Yeah? I feel like I've been hit by a two ton Brahma. But I was laughing at how happy Gypsy and Blue were to see each other." He had a thought. "Where's Sadie?"

Dean grinned like a fool. "Sleeping in there with Daddy. He likes the window open, summer and winter, and Miss Sadie likes to sniff."

"Ah. I was wondering." She hadn't come to greet him, but the old girl didn't hear well anymore, so if she was asleep, she'd not know. He'd give the old girl her treats in the morning. Treats. Oh!

"I got you some of those pralines you like."

"Oh, you did? I picked you up some new jeans at the Wal-Mart. You said you were needing."

Always taking care of him. "Did you get the stuff for cobbler? I've a mind to spoil you and your daddy some."

Those cheeks heated. "Peaches and blackberries both. 'nilla ice cream, too."

Will kissed first one cheek then the other. "Perfect. I'll start tomorrow."

"Mmmhmm. Tonight we'll be easy in our bones and maybe have a nice shower."

"Oh, that sounds like heaven if you've got hot water." That sounded like better than heaven, actually. Just. Yeah. Will grinned. "Love you, cowboy."

"Love you, Ace. Sleep a little. I'll wake you in a bit for a bite and a soak."

"Okay." Hell. He'd been driving for days. And Dean needed the rest, too. So he just snuggled in, letting his eyes droop. They had time. Time for everything he wanted to say and do.

Later.

"You want some more cobbler, Daddy?"

Dean watched Daddy nod off, head bobbing over the table, and he winked at Will. Lord in Heaven, it made it easier, having Will right there, smiling, watching. Being. "If you'll clear the table, Ace? I'll get him settled for the night."

"You bet. I think he liked supper, Dean." Will got up, easy as anything, one hand resting on his daddy's shoulder for a moment before Will moved to the sink and started filling it with water and soap.

"Come on, old man. Bedtime."

Daddy looked up, frowned a little. "Already? But it's just dark."

"I know, but you're sleeping already. Let's get you settled and you can watch a movie or something..."

Those green eyes stared him down. "You just want time with your young man."

"Yes. So cooperate and go to bed and I'll drive you up to Greenville for a beer sometime next week."

Cantankerous old bastard.

He heard a chuckle, Will coming to get the plates. "Heck, we get you set with the movie and you promise to take those meds, and I'll run out and get you some beer tomorrow. Some of that fancy stuff you like. How about She Wore a Yellow Ribbon?"

"Oh, I like him, son. You should keep him."

Dean nodded, grinned, winked over at Will who was blushing dark. "That's the general idea, Daddy. Come on, bathroom and I'll get your pills."

To his everlasting surprise, his daddy went easily, right to the bathroom and then to bed, sitting up with his remote in his fancy bed. He got the movie started, and by the time he got back to the kitchen it was neat as a pin, the dishes done.

"You all right, cowboy?"

"Yeah, doing good. Thanks for supper, Ace. It was something else." He went over, got himself a kiss, not thinking about the fact that Will'd be leaving soon.

"I know how you like roast and rice and gravy. And cobbler." Will kissed him right back, hands sliding to cup his ass, just holding on. "And it makes me happy to do it."

"Oh, it's nice to have you home." He leaned up, lips wandering a little, just jonesing on the little bit of salt, little bit of musk.

"Mmmhmm." Giving it right back, Will nuzzled his skin, licking and nibbling. Just loving on him.

His fingers walked right up along Will's belly, searching out those tight, hard little nipples.

"Oh, Dean. Yeah. Feels good." Those strong hands tucked into his back pockets, squeezing, digging right into his muscles.

He groaned, the sound all raw and rough, all about needing. "You... Lord, you're something else."

"You think I am? I think you're the keeper, cowboy." Grinning, Will just sorta danced them out of the kitchen. "We need to sit."

"I'm good at sitting. Front room or bedroom?" He got himself a nibble, getting at the curve of Will's jaw.

"Bedroom. Just in case."

Yeah, it wasn't likely Daddy would be up and about, but there was no sense giving him a free show if he was.

"Mmm... yeah." They two-stepped down the hall, nice and easy, moving like it was the most natural thing on Earth.

They always danced damned well together.

"Just gonna..." Will worked at his shirt, opening buttons. Then Will attacked his jeans.

"Will, you make me want." His cock was just pushing, trying to get Will's attention, Will's touch.

"Good. God, cowboy." It worked. Will's hand closed around him, warm and callused, scraping right against his skin, setting it ablaze. "You feel like nothing else, ever."

He leaned against the wall, hips pumping, rocking up into Will's hand. Fuck. Sweet fuck, Will made him feel young.

"Gotta." Will pushed him harder against the wall and dropped down in front of him, stubbly cheek rubbing on his cock before that tongue slipped out to taste him.

He went up on his toes, thighs going rock-hard and tight. The textured wall scraped against his back, rough as all get out and didn't that just make things better?

A soft noise vibrated all the way down to his balls, Will's hand sliding under them and lifting them. Lips tight around him, Will started sucking, just bobbing up and down.

"I. Love. Oh. Will." He finally stopped trying to make sense, just worried about feeling and watching and loving.

Those blue, blue eyes opened, looked right up at him as Will sucked him in, encouraging him on. So hot, watching those tanned cheeks hollow out.

His breath sort of huffed out of him, all rough and husky, balls tighter than fuck. He opened his mouth to warn Will he couldn't wait, but his body was a step ahead, pouring right into that hot, hungry mouth.

Will took him right down without a sound, just petting his hip, cradling his balls. Tongue catching the very last of him, Will pulled back, grinning up. "Now that? That's a good look for you, cowboy."

Dean chuckled, blinked down and sort of nodded. "I. Damn. 's good."

"Uh huh." Will got up, hand sliding behind his neck, pulling him over for a kiss. "Real good."

Oh, damn. He could taste himself, right there, right in

Will's mouth.

Damn.

The kiss went deep, Will just fucking his mouth with that sweet tongue, taking it. Will pressed against him, rubbing, needing. He got his fingers to work, popped those faded jeans right open, hunting flesh. All the while Will was making his head swim, stealing his breath clean away.

"Oh." Pulling away to gasp that single word, Will breathed on his lips, hot and good as Will's cock pushed right into his hand. "Oh, please, cowboy."

"Want in, Will? Want me?" He stroked, good and hard, loving on his Will with all he was.

"You know it, Dean. Know I do." Yeah, he could feel the jump in Will's pulse, hear it in the catch in Will's voice. They moved, careful like thanks to their clothes and his hold on Will, right to the bed so they could get comfy.

He found the little tube of stuff while Will was stripping down, his own prick starting to come back to life, take a little notice.

Will crawled up on the bed, all legs and tanned skin, the white around his hips and ass startling, emphasizing the curve of those hard muscles. Cock bobbing, Will held out a hand, waiting.

He took himself a second, got a long look, then went where it was he needed to go. "Damn, Ace. Need you bone deep."

"I know." The hard lines etched by Will's mouth said more than the words. So did the fine tremor of Will's hand as he took the tube. "It hurts sometimes how much."

"C'mere and love me." He licked at those lines, at those lips, before settling on hands and knees, just giving it up for his Will.

"Hell, yes." Will fumbled a bit, but soon enough those long fingers pushed at him, slick and hot. Stretching him carefully, Will moved up close, heat radiating against his hip, the wet tip of Will's cock sliding.

Low sounds slipped from him and his legs went all tight, trembly. Oh, Lord yes. He was needing. "Yeah. Yeah, feels good."

"Tight." Oh, Will sounded strained, voice rough and low. Finally those fingers slipped out and Will moved up behind him, hands on his back, fingers tracing the scars as Will's cock probed him. "Love."

"Oh, Hell, yes." He just sort of leaned back and let Will on in, a dull heat making a ball in his belly.

In no time Will had slid right home, hips up against Dean's ass, hands hard on his hips. Will didn't say a word, just panted, cock riding in and out of him, opening him up so good.

He stared down at his hands, twisted all up in the quilt. His quilt. His hands. His cowboy in him. Sweet Jesus. Dean groaned, rocked back a little harder, toes curling as he rode.

"Damn, cowboy. Damn." Faster and faster, Will rocked him, their skin slapping. Leaning down, Will kissed his back, lips touching on every scar, every line.

"Yeah." Man, his breath just huffed from him, a drop of sweat slip-sliding down his nose. Sweet Christ, Will was gonna make him go-round again they weren't careful.

So good. Will gasped against him again, hips pushing and pushing, and he felt it. Felt that very moment when Will came inside him. His eyes closed and he just felt it, felt Will. He leaned down to press his lips to Will's hand, that fine fucking hand on his quilt, fingers starting to shake.

"Oh, Dean." Yeah. He could hear it in Will's voice, too. What they weren't saying. Not at all.

Sometimes there wasn't any call for talking, not when

a man could feel.

Will sighed, setting his bag down by the door and getting ready to put his boots on. He hadn't wanted to make coffee or noise for fear of waking Dean's daddy. The man had drunk down some beers with them and stayed up too late watching movies and Will didn't want to disturb.

So he went out to the truck after his boots were on and got everything hitched up right and... waited for Dean. He needed that last minute or two of his cowboy before he hit the road and called himself all manner of a fool on down the road a few miles.

Dean brought Gypsy around, loaded her up. Blueboy was stomping and tossing his head, just raising a ruckus and pouting to beat the band. Those grey eyes met his, a little blood-shot from last night, but still just right. "He don't want her to go. He's spoiled."

"We all are." He got a smile up, just working it for Dean. "I'll be back with her as soon as I can, though. I thought I'd swing through again before I head up to Kansas."

"I'd like that. You know I'll be here." Waiting. Just as sad and patient as all get out.

His constant. His cowboy. "I know. You'll make sure you and your daddy eat that cobbler I left in the freezer? I know how he likes the blueberry, even if it does stain so."

"I will. You take care of that leg, now, okay? I worry on it." Dean's fingers stroked his wrist, right above his watch. "And call if you want, collect even."

"I will." Yeah. He would call. A lot. "I got me one of those pay ahead cards at the Wal-Mart."

"Good. Gonna..." Dean swallowed, boot scuffing at a weed, the dust billowing a bit. "Was damn good to see you, Will. Damn good."

His hand automatically moved, going to touch Dean's cheek. The morning stubble scraped his palm. "It was. We'll do it again soon. Promise. No one makes better coffee'n you do."

"You just ride, cowboy. Me and Miss Sadie'll keep things quiet here."

He grinned. It sure had taken Sadie longer to warm to him this time than it had Dean. She'd been not talking to him at all for two days. Grumpy old broad.

"I'll do the best I can." He'd send as much back to Dean as he could, too. There were some repairs that just took money that Dean didn't have with his daddy and all. That, if nothing else, stiffened his resolve to head on back out.

"You always do." Dean nodded, fingers squeezing his a second. "Get on, now, 'fore I forget myself and hold on."

"Come here and give me a kiss first." Damned if he was leaving without that. He pulled Dean close, settling his mouth right under that mustache, kissing gently.

Dean's hand landed on his waist, thumb drawing circles as they just breathed together for a minute, eyes watching him close. "Love you, you know, yeah?"

"I know. Same here, cowboy." His lashes felt damned sticky when he blinked. "Well, I'd best get on."

"Yeah, you'll be wanting to make Abilene. You take care now." Dean stepped back, finger stroking some dust off the truck, looking back at Gypsy. "Keep him outta trouble, girl."

They both laughed when Gypsy snorted, kicking the trailer.

Lord. He checked everything one last time, moving

close enough to touch the small of Dean's back, lingering just a moment before he headed for the cab of the truck. "I'll call when I get to the campground. You keep it going, cowboy."

He couldn't quite meet Dean's eyes as he hopped in and put the truck in gear.

But he sure could see Dean watching him go in the rearview mirror.

Twelve

The nurses all knew him, nodded and spoke right friendly. Hell, Ken the Orderly smoked with him in the courtyard at noon Thursday through Monday, regular as clockwork.

It was funny, how the things the people said changed when the end came close. "I hope he feels better" turned to "He's headed for a better place." "Chin up" became "We'll pray for you."

He didn't believe that Daddy was still in there, not really. There'd been a minute, three days ago, where Daddy'd blinked, looked at him, but it hadn't lasted and now?

Now it was time to go home. Time for all of them to.

Dean leaned over, kissed the cool forehead. "Momma's waiting, now. You'd best get on. Don't worry 'bout them calves, I'll bring 'em in. Keep 'em safe and home. You got my word, Daddy."

He was home and he'd take care.

Damn it. Will sighed and straightened his tie, taking his hat off as he walked up to the very fringe of the circle of people around the casket. They were lowering it, everyone looking solemn and sad.

He'd missed Joe's funeral, made it just in time for the tail end of the graveside service, and he'd be damned if he'd elbow in. Hell, he was lucky Dean'd caught him at all. He'd gotten the message at the arena day before yesterday and had driven fourteen hours to get there.

He'd just have to do his comforting after.

Dean was standing there in front with his brother Allen. Funny how two brothers only four years apart could look so very different. Allen looked like an all-star quarterback gone to pot next to Dean, who'd done nothing but gotten leaner in the last couple months. It would be easy to growl and frown at the man, if he hadn't been more busy and distracted than mean.

Even after all the bad feelings, Allen'd been the one who told Joe to give all the land to Dean, that it was the right thing to do. Allen'd even paid for the hospital stay, in the end, saying Dean would need the rest of the life insurance for seed money on the farm.

Dean had on a black hat, black shirt and jeans and managed to look normal and somber all at once. There were almost a hundred folks gathered around, too -- cowboys and nurses, church people and farmers -- all paying respect.

It was good folks had turned out. Joe'd been a good man, even though he'd not been all there once Will got to know him. But it would mean a lot to Dean.

He thought about the stuff he had packed away in the Chevy, and it occurred to him that maybe Dean wouldn't need him to make supper, not if the church ladies had. Still, he wanted to do something, anything, to make up for not being there.

Dean's chin lifted, those eyes wandering, lost right up until they found him. Then, he got a nod, a quirk of those lips and he'd be damned if the stiffness in those shoulders didn't ease some.

He nodded right back, waiting until some of the hand shaking was over and Allen moved away before he went on over.

"Hey cowboy. How's it hanging?"

"Been a long, long few days. Didn't expect to see you 'til tomorrow, if at all, Ace." Dean looked maybe fifty years old, grey. "So glad you're here."

"I drove straight through. Sorry I'm late." He reached out, touched the back of Dean's hand and shut his mouth. This wasn't about him. "I got some groceries. Thought you might be hankering for some green chile stew and tortillas after all the macaroni and cheese and chicken casserole."

Dean nodded, head down, voice so low. "What I want? Is for all these nice folks to go on and let me and you have some rest."

"Well, then, that's what we'll ask for." He smiled at the lady walking toward them and took Dean by the elbow, steering him off the other way. "Whyn't you go sit in the truck, or say hi to Gypsy, and I'll tell Allen."

Dean blinked over at him, heading right for the trailer, easy as anything. "You don't mind?"

"Not a bit. Go on, cowboy." Will split off halfway, heading over to Dean's brother. "Hey there. Do you mind if I take Dean on home? He's needing some time. Pooped right out."

Allen sighed, nodded. "How about I direct everyone over to the meeting hall? Patty and I can bring the food over in the morning. The boys will want to spend some time with Dean."

"You betcha." He held out a hand. "I sure am sorry,

Allen."

"It was time. He... I know you don't think I cared, but this was hurting Dean, too." His hand was taken, squeezed. "I'm glad you came out."

Will squeezed back. "You're a good man, Allen. And I do appreciate all you've done. I know Dean does. Thank you, for handling the crowd. We'll see you folks tomorrow."

Lord, he felt bad now, didn't he? Poor Allen.

Will headed back to the brother who needed him, though, without a backward glance.

Dean wasn't in the truck, but he could see boots through the trailer, his cowboy leaning into Gypsy, just holding on that chestnut mare.

"Hey, cowboy? You ready? Allen's taking the rest of the folks to the meeting hall. He says he'll see you tomorrow."

Dean needed a bath. A meal. Some coddling.

So did Will. He needed to do for Dean.

Dean cleared his throat, patting Gypsy's flank. "Yeah. Yeah. I'm ready. I want to go home."

"Well, we're burning daylight." Hitching the trailer back up after Dean, Will headed around to the driver's side, sliding in and turning to touch Dean's cheek. "Love you, cowboy. You know that, yeah?"

"Yeah. Let's go." Dean buckled up, one hand on his knee. "I'm sure glad to see you."

"Same here, cowboy." God, Dean had bags under his eyes that had bags of their own. "So, how's Sadie taking it? She missing him still?"

Dean'd said the old dog looked for Joe for days after he went in the hospital.

"You know it. She just sort of wanders." Dean sighed. "Blueboy's going real good, though. Looking fat and sassy."

"Lazy old bastard. I got Sadie some of them soft sausage treats, and an apple for Blue, so we can spoil 'em."

The ride just took forever. He wanted to pull over and put his arms around Dean and hold on. But he drove, and they got there, and he killed the engine, looking at the old house, admiring how Dean had worked on sprucing it up.

"He must've been so proud, Dean."

"I think he felt settled at the end, you know? I think he was okay to leave it to me." Dean's eyes wandered, just moving over things. "I can't believe it's over."

Shit. Will hopped out and walked right around, opening Dean's door and opening his arms. "C'mere."

Dean did, just came right over and let them have what they needed, no bullshit, no drama.

They kissed, lips moving on cheeks and lips and chins, slow, easy kisses. Will held Dean close, swaying, their belt buckles catching. Dean sort of leaned into him, took each kiss and made it linger, made it last.

Wrapping one hand around Dean's neck, Will turned them, leaning back against the truck and propping them up. He stroked Dean's poor back with his other hand, feeling how tense Dean was. How tired.

"How long can you stay?" Dean's hand moved slow and easy on his belly.

"I got a couple weeks before I drop too far in the standings. I'd stay out the rest of the season and the off, but I got a chance at the twenty-five thousand at Mesquite, and we could sure use that."

"Oh, man. You and Gypsy can stay here for that one too and I'll come cheer you on." Dean found him a real, honest-to-god smile. "It's been too long since I got to see you work."

That was what he wanted for sure. That smile. He

smoothed Dean's mustache with his thumb. "You bet. Between now and then I need to hit a few of the major events, though."

No sense sugar coating. "Now, how do you feel about Mexican food?"

"Shit, Will. At this point I just don't wanna ever see another hospital tray again."

"I bet. That Jell-o shit is scary." Inside. He needed to get Dean inside and get Gypsy settled. "You want to take the bags in while I settle this lady? I'll meet you there."

"Yeah. Did I give you keys for the lock last time?"

"You did." He grinned, kissing Dean one more time. "We'll get what has to be done doing, then we'll hit the couch, yeah?"

Heaven was an old chintz sofa for sure.

"You know it." Dean smiled over, nodded. "I'll meet you there."

The work took minutes and he begrudged it, but that was what you did. You got the critters settled. He said hi to Blueboy, gave him the apple, got Gypsy fed and set and locked in tight, and then went back to Dean.

Who was feeding Sadie a Snausage.

Sadie wagged and barked for him, leaving the treat to push her nose into his hand, give him a lick.

Oh. "Hey, lady. Come here and love on me." He knelt, let her snuffle his face. God. He was the biggest idiot on earth sometimes, leaving this. Her tags jingled as he rubbed her scruff back and forth.

Dean watched them, pulling off the dress boots Will knew pinched his toes, working the buttons on the too-new black shirt.

"There's my cowboy." Knees popping, Will got up, went over to sit on the couch. "Want some of you, Dean. Come sit?"

Dean nodded, coming over and sitting close, just

leaning against him. “Hey, Ace.”

“Hey.” Putting an arm around Dean, Will pulled him tight to his side, kissing gently. They sat for the longest time, soaking each other in.

“Thank you.” The words were so soft, so gentle, just breathed against his lips.

“Anytime, cowboy. Any old time at all.”

Thirteen

The night had never been longer. It was maybe three am, and you couldn't cut the dark with a knife when Will pulled up to Dean's little house. God he was tired. All the way down. Hell, even his toes were cramping, because his old second or third or fourth hand truck didn't have cruise control, and he'd been pushing that accelerator all the way from Wichita Falls.

Now, though, he was kinda afraid to go in there. He had a key, but damned if he didn't feel like he ought to knock. Will folded his hands on the steering wheel and bent his head down, resting a minute. He should maybe just sleep in the truck, not wake Dean up. Lord knew Dean had enough on his plate and he wasn't expecting Will back anyway, since he was supposed to be on the road to Amarillo.

His ankle was just too bad, though, and he didn't have the money to make entry fees until he paid off the emergency room bill in Oklahoma City, so he needed to do some odd jobs, spend a little time working. Goddamn, he sounded like a pathetic asshole. He should get up and get his ass in there.

A tap came on the window, grey eyes looking in, warm, sympathetic. "Bed's more comfortable than the truck, Ace. I'll put Gypsy in the barn. Coffee's brewing."

Oh. Will blinked hard, nodding. "Sorry. I'd do her up, but I'm a gimp."

"My gimp. I'll keep you." Dean opened the door, took the keys from the ignition to go unlock the trailer. As Dean moved back, that soft, soft mustache brushed his cheek.

Sometimes a man just didn't know how much he needed something, someone, until he was right there. Will grabbed his crutches out of the passenger side and clumped into the house. Least he could do was get the coffee ready for when Dean came back in, and maybe a plate of something. Eggs. Sandwiches. Something.

He got the cups down, the smell of brewing coffee making his mouth actually water. Damn. He should have gotten something back at his last rest stop. He piled bread in the toaster and put eggs on to fry.

The kitchen was simple, clean. Dean had pulled down the paneling, painted the walls a pale yellow, the cabinets edged with blue.

It didn't take Dean long before the back door opened up, mud knocked off the old work boots. "You go sit, Ace. I'll finish up. You look rode hard."

"I'm afraid if I sit I won't get up again." He grinned over, Dean's very presence easing him. Despite his words he eased right into a kitchen chair, sticking that damned throbbing ankle right out in front of him. His damned leg never would work right.

"You can sit a spell. I won't mind." Dean turned the eggs before he grabbed a couple tea towels and an ice pack from the freezer. "Let's get your boot off, Ace, and get things better. Ice and heat, yeah?"

There was the sting again, making him blink some more, making him so damned glad to be right where he was. He eased his boot off, groaning at the release of the pressure. "You're damned good to me, Dean. How'd you know I was home?"

"Miss Sadie went to barking when you pulled up. Not long, mind you, but she noticed." The ice pack settled on his ankle, then his eggs and toast were set in front of him. "You want milk?"

"No, this is good. Sit with me?" He reached for Dean's hand, holding him there when he would have puttered some more.

One rough hand cupped his jaw, thumb rubbing his chin. Those eyes were staring at him like he was Christmas and birthday all at once. "Hey."

"Hey." He smiled up, turning his face down so he could kiss Dean's hand, just letting the last few days fall away. "Been missing you, cowboy."

"You've had a rough couple. You getting to stay a day or two? Let me heal you up?"

"I am. Probably a few weeks, the doc was right about the ankle. He didn't want me driving, but I wanted to come home." He should eat while the eggs were hot, and Will made himself dig in because his stomach was empty as a worm. "Needed you."

Dean moved around behind him, hands working his shoulders good and hard. "Oh. A couple of weeks sounds like Heaven."

"Yeah." He let his head drop forward, let the last scrap of toast sit. "Kitchen looks amazing. How've you been, cowboy?"

"Missing my better half, but staying busy. Bought thirty head of cattle and a Beefmaster bull. Rode fence. Been doing a little roofing work when the opportunity presented itself."

He leaned back in his chair, into Dean's hands, his own hands going back to stroke Dean's legs. Damn his own stubborn hide anyway, he should just stay. But he had a few good rides left in him, and he'd hate to miss out on that too. Will just gave up thinking and let Dean take the load off, just for a bit.

"Mmm... Let me grab the heating pad and we'll get your sweet ass to bed. You needing a shower tonight or will it wait til morning?"

"It can wait." He'd cleaned up good before the pain had finally sent him to the damned doctor and he'd rather snuggle with Dean than just about anything.

"Good." His plate was taken, slid into the sink. The ice pack was taken off, put back in the freezer, then a square hand was offered over. "Come to bed, Will."

"Sounds good." He levered up, grabbed one crutch so he could hobble on, but he stopped long enough to kiss Dean hello before they moved. Oh. Oh, yeah.

Dean smiled, the kiss deep and slow. "Bed. Now. Off that foot."

"Okay, cowboy." They managed to get to the bedroom with without falling down, and there was Miss Sadie. It was sad, how she just didn't get around much, but he had a smile for her and she had a wagging tail for him, and he petted her a bit before slumping on the bed and just watching Dean.

Dean got his other boot off, then undressed him and got him settled, ankle resting on a heating pad and pillow, sweet as you please. Then Dean stripped down, turning off lights and loving on Sadie before sliding in.

Will reached for him, needing to feel Dean's skin, Dean's weight against his side after too many lonely nights. He moaned as Dean scooted up against him. "Much better."

"You know it." Dean's hands started roaming, exploring, sliding over him, just so.

Warm. Good. Dean. Will turned a little, careful of his ankle, searching blindly for Dean's mouth.

Oh, yeah. The kiss wasn't earth-shattering, but it was so good, so warm, so... Dean.

Home. Will went searching for Dean's taste, tongue pushing in, slow and easy. Coffee and spice and everything he needed right then and there. Dean cupped his head, tilted him and took the kiss deep, making his head spin.

He could just have that a good long while. Will opened up, let Dean taste him just as good, hands coming up to pet Dean's shoulders, search out the scars on Dean's back.

That got him a low moan, Dean scooting closer, cock hard and hot where it pressed against him.

"Yeah. Oh, yeah, cowboy." They shifted, pressed together, and Will couldn't believe how damned good that felt. Amazing, what this man did to him. He rested one hand on Dean's hip, the other tracing Dean's cheek, his lips, cupping his chin to bring him in for another kiss, then another.

"Yeah." Dean petted his belly, rubbing against him. They loved on each other, Will touching and touching, just needing so bad. Dean's lips moved down his body, mustache tickling his skin.

Will arched up, hands massaging Dean's shoulders, muscles going all tight. God, he loved that mustache. "Dean. Oh, cowboy."

"Yeah. Need to taste you, Will. Make sure I remember right."

"Uh huh. Yeah." Okay, he was about to start babbling any minute. Will shifted onto his back, spread his legs, careful to just move the uninjured one, giving Dean easy access. "Please."

Dean's hand cupped his balls, rolling them nice and slow. That mustache dragged up along his shaft and then his cock was taken into pure heat.

"Shit!" Yeah. Oh, God yeah. Will thrust up before he

thought, then pressed back against the bed, not wanting to push too hard. "Good."

Dean's hands pressed him down into the mattress, "Be still."

Then Dean took him again, sucking hard.

Be still. Right, when he felt like he was on a bronc, his whole body trying to buck. He shook, the muscles in belly and thighs quivering, his cock just throbbing.

Dean stroked and sucked, loving on him like no one else. Ever.

He tried hard to stay in one place, tried not to wiggle and hump, but damn. Oh, damn. He petted Dean's back and shoulders and arms.

He looked down, Dean's eyes were closed, his cowboy looked like all was right with his world.

Dean's skin was warm, lean muscles moving under his fingers, and Will figured there was no place he'd rather be. His hips started rolling, fighting Dean's grip, trying to get more.

Dean's hands slid up under his ass, pulling him in deeper.

"Oh! Oh, cowboy." That was it; that was all it took. Will shot hard, a hoarse cry tearing out, his hips just snapping.

Dean kept licking and tasting until he was clean and melted.

"So good, Will."

"Mmm. Yeah. C'mere cowboy." He felt so good, easy in his bones, all the tension drained right out. He wanted kisses.

Dean cuddled right up close, fingers petting and loving him, those lips hot and soft.

He kissed those lips, opening them with his, tongue sliding in, just a little, his hand reaching for Dean's cock.

Dean moaned, hips sliding to push into his touch.

"Will. Ace."

"So hot, Dean." That skin was so hot, thin and velvety over hardness. Will stroked, hand closing tight, pulling.

Dean made a low, raw sound, grey eyes rolling. Beautiful. He wanted more of that, more sounds, more of Dean's hot breath. Will went faster and faster, mouth closing on Dean's throat, sucking.

Hotter than a two dollar pistol, Dean just gave it up to him, heat splashing on his wrist in no time.

"Cowboy. Love." Will leaned in, kissed the moan right off Dean's lips, loving this man so much it hurt.

"Yeah." Dean pressed close, hands petting him, stroking.

Will wrapped one arm around Dean and settled, getting comfy enough to sleep the rest of the night away, what there was of it. "Don't worry, cowboy. I'll be here when you wake up."

Dean chuckled. "And I'll be out feeding the horses when you wake up. Sleep, Ace."

"'Kay." He'd make it up to Dean tomorrow. With a cobbler. And some loving. And he'd stay a few weeks. Will smiled. He was already looking forward to it.

Dean dragged himself up and out of the bed only a bit later than normal. He started coffee, got Will's laundry going, the trailer swept out. Critters fed and Gypsy's feet cleaned. Then he called up Mr. Pecina down at the tack shop, arranging some work on Will's saddle.

He knew Will'd get on him about being an old woman, but he didn't get to take care often.

Miss Sadie was sleeping on the porch in a sunbeam, looking as peaceful as could be, as he headed in to reckon breakfast.

The clump of crutches on the floor preceded Will, and damned if Ace didn't look funny as hell, naked and flopping about as he swung on those crutches. There was nothing funny about that bright smile and those sweet blue eyes, though. "Hey, cowboy."

"Mornin', Ace." He grinned, went for his kiss. "You get good rest?"

Will gave the kiss easily, lips a little swollen from last night. "You bet. Better than I have in an age."

"Good to hear it." Dean couldn't help but touch, not with it right there and offered so pretty.

"Mmm. Good way to work up an appetite for breakfast."

"You know it." He leaned in, breathed deep, smiled at the scent that was more familiar than breathing.

Will's crutches toppled to the kitchen floor, those long arms going around his neck as Will pressed against him, kissed him.

He cupped Will's ass, supporting, holding, bracing them both as they swayed.

Soft, sweet noises met his touch, Will rubbing against him, and he could feel that hard cock through the denim of his jeans.

"Mmm..." Oh, sweet Jesus, yes. The kiss got hard, hungry, Will meeting him more than halfway.

Those strong, rough hands felt so good on him, pulling his shirt up out of his waistband, sliding under to trace the scars on his back.

"Oh, nothing like your hands, Will. Nothing in Heaven or Earth."

"Yeah? I was just thinking there was nothing like your mouth, Dean. Or your skin." Will grinned, swaying a little as that leg gave.

"Let's take this somewhere you can relax, yeah? Somewhere you can have both."

"Sounds good, cowboy." They got Will turned around, got him headed back toward the bedroom, but Will veered off in the front room, flopping on the sofa. "Damn."

He chuckled, ended on his knees between Will's legs. "Yeah. Damn."

"Mmm. Yeah. Hey there." Will cupped his cheek, thumb rubbing over his lips.

He sucked that thumb in, hands sliding along those long, long legs.

The fine hairs on the insides of Will's thighs caught on his fingers, and Will's cock rose between those legs, red and hard and hot. Will moaned, wet thumb tracing his mouth again, getting his lips good and wet. "Love you how you look when you taste me, Dean."

"Good." He leaned in for a kiss, for a nice, long taste.

Will was all over it, kissing, touching, working at getting to his skin. It took a bit, but he got naked, rubbing against Will, just purring with it. So decadent, making love in the front room with the sun pouring in.

"C'mere." Will turned, bad foot on the floor, the other up along the back of the couch, pulling him up on top. "Want to feel you."

He damn near whimpered, seeing Will spread out like a pie supper. "Damn, Will. You're something else."

"You're the special one, cowboy. Love the way you feel." Will petted, stroked, bit his neck.

They fit, hand in glove, and it wasn't anything to start rocking, rubbing them together. They rubbed, Will pulling him until their cocks came together, their kisses getting wild, heavy and hot. He had one hand braced on the sofa, the other on Will's ass, keeping them close and tight.

So good. Will had one hand on his back, fingers

stroking, the other on his thigh, pulling so they got even more friction.

He met Will's eyes, loving the happiness there, the way the tired lines were already fading, already disappearing.

"Come on, cowboy. Come on." Will just smiled at him, held him, loved on him.

"Uhn..." He nodded, tumbling over the edge, easy as anything.

Took maybe two more thrusts for Will to come right along with him, that long prick jerking against his, feel it sliding over his belly.

"Oh. Oh, now, that's just right." He took a kiss, all about smiling.

"You know it. You make everything good, lover."

Oh, he did like the way that sounded. "It's what I'm for, holding up my better half."

"Hey, I'm holding you up." Will laughed, nuzzling into his throat. "You take care of Gypsy? Man, I feel bad the state she was in. Makes me ashamed."

"I did. Cleaned her feet up, gave her a B-6 shot and a brushing. Got your saddle down to the Pecina's, too. He'll put it to rights."

"Oh." Squeezing him tight, Will sighed, but it was a happy sound. "You're good to me. I owe you a cobbler."

"I'll hold you to it." He leaned down, nuzzling. "How's that ankle feeling?"

"Better, with you doctoring me." Will belied that a little by shifting, that foot coming up to rest on the couch along his leg.

"We'll get you right as rain, you just wait." And if he hoped it didn't pass too quick? Well, the good Lord would keep that secret.

"I know. I can always count on you, cowboy." Guilt had crept into Will's voice, and that? Wasn't gonna do.

"Hey, now." He met Will's eyes. "This old man? Ain't

going nowhere. You ride and I'll hold the fort for after. That was the deal."

"I know." Will nodded, leaned up to kiss his chin. "And I'm not ready to throw it in yet, but I miss the Hell out of you."

"Yeah. I hear that." He nodded, smiled. "But better to miss me now than hate me later. You want to ride down to the Broken B, get some biscuits and gravy?"

"Hell, yes. And for the record? I can't ever imagine hating you." Will kissed him again, patted his bare ass. "Just let me get clothes and crutches."

"Oh, let's get us both in the shower first." He felt his cheeks heat. "I... I put in a new shower head..."

A fancy removable massaging one.

"Yeah? Now that? Sounds like a plan."

"Yeah." He angled himself up, helped Will along. "Yeah, it sure does."

Maybe the showerhead went a little farther than the mother henning. But damn, it was gonna be fun.

Fourteen

He shut the front door, plopped down on the sofa and sighed. He could hear the quiet all around him, heavy and sticky as the dog days and he...

He needed, even if it was just a quick call. Even if it was just a minute.

Dean grabbed the phone and dialed, praying that Will had the cell on, that Ace picked up.

"'Lo?" Sure enough, Will picked up on the second ring, staticky and far away, but there.

"Hey, stranger. How goes it?" Thank you, God.

"Hey! Better now, I can tell you. How're you, cowboy?"

"Been a long day. You on the road?"

"Yeah. I... well," Will chuckled. "I was thinking about skipping Denton and one of the Mesquite dates and just... coming home for a bit."

"Yeah? I..." Dean nodded, fingers tight on the phone. "I'd like that, Will. I'd like that a lot."

"So would I. A lot. I don't stop tonight I could be home soon enough." Ace sounded hopeful. And damned tired.

"You don't push it too hard, yeah? There's a blue norther due in tomorrow 'round noon; it breaks early, it could make for shit driving." Oh. Home. Tomorrow. Oh. His heart ached just thinking on it.

"Then it makes more sense to push hard." The chuckle was back again. It had gotten to where he and Will had that argument a good bit. Will said there was no sense lollygagging about now that Dean wasn't traveling with him. Didn't have anything to stay at a nice hotel for, or camp for a week.

He grinned -- damned near hurt his face. "You sure you remember where your old man is? How to get home?"

"God. Yeah. I think about it, and you, every damned minute of the day." Something in that familiar voice told Dean there wasn't an ounce of joke to be found. Serious as a heart attack.

He nodded, voice all choked up. "Come home, Will. I... Doc Trumble had me put Sadie down this morning. It's damned quiet here."

I need you.

The fragile link connecting them was quiet for long, long moments, then Will's voice was there again, easing the knot in his chest. "I'll be home before morning, cowboy. You just leave a light on for me, you hear?"

"I'll be waiting. You bring yourself on safe to me, Ace."

"You know it. Put on some music in the meantime, okay? Or one of those bad westerns you like so much." The kid knew him too well, knew he'd need the noise.

"Yeah. I'll find a good movie at the store. I reckon I'll make a grocery run so we won't starve." He found another smile, a real one, one that felt good. "'sides, I haven't had a good cobbler in ages."

"Make sure you got milk, then, and whatever kind of fruit you want in it, and I'll bake you one up tomorrow. I." sounded like Will was kinda choked, too. "I miss you,

Dean. I'm coming home."

"Good. I'll make sure there's a stall cleaned for Gyspy and a warm spot for you in our bed." He stood up, reached for his hat. "See you in a few, Will."

"Soon as can be, Dean." The silence drew out again, neither of them willing to say goodbye.

He finally just whispered "Soon, Ace. Soon" and headed to the old Chevy, headed for town.

Soon.

It was raining like crazy by the time Will got home. He sloshed around and got Gypsy put up and dry and happy and unloaded most of his gear, figuring Dean would be asleep this late, or early, however you looked at it.

Damn, he was tired. Even more than he had been, after talking to Dean, and he needed to see the man, to touch him, 'cause that was the only thing that would ease him.

He hit the porch and eased his boots off, no sense tracking mud all over, before tiptoeing in, smiling when he saw the lamp on the hall table had been left on for him.

"You want some coffee, stranger? That wind sounds cold." The voice came from the front room, Dean sitting up from the sofa, rumpled and just waking.

"Coffee sounds like a damned good idea." 'Course there were other things that warmed a body up, and Will hung his jacket up before heading over to the best one in the world, planting his hand on the back of the couch and kissing Dean hello.

Familiar, missed hands wrapped over his shoulders and pulled him in close, Dean giving a quiet, needy little sound as their lips met.

Damn. Too long. He'd been gone too long this time, trying to get his points in on the circuit so he could spend a good long while at home. The kiss only broke when he figured he was gonna pass out from lack of air, and Will plopped down next to Dean on the sofa. "Hey."

"Hey." He got a slow smile, Dean's eyes a little shadowed, a little tired. "How was the drive?"

"Long. But the weather held until about twenty minutes from home." Will got up and pulled Dean up with him, heading for the bedroom. "Coffee can wait."

Dean nodded, right on his heels. The bed was made, the ceiling fan blowing slow and easy and oh...

Dean's hands fell on his shoulder, massaging. Rubbing.

"Oh. Damn, that's good Dean." Will stood stock still for a minute and let Dean work the sore out. Ever since he'd dislocated the thing on that ornery mustang he rode in Ruidoso on the New Mexico circuit in the spring, well, it got sore in the wet.

Lips brushed his nape, those strong hands working him hard. "Feels good, Will."

"Mmm." He gave Dean another minute or two to do for him before turning and taking those rough hands in his, pulling the man in for another kiss. He needed. That taste, that smell, the feel of the man hard against him. Needed it bad.

Dean's fingers twined with his as they kissed, holding on tight, the grip telling him how much he'd been needed, been missed.

God, it was usually hard, but it seemed worse than ever this time, had even before Dean'd called. They needed to talk. But later, after they got over the storm of loving they were about to be in the middle of. Will pushed his tongue into Dean's mouth, pushing the man himself back to the bed until their legs hit, toppling them over.

Dean groaned, loosening up on one hand to tug at his shirt, search for skin.

He went for skin, too, scrabbling at Dean's shirt, moaning when his fingers hit the softsoft skin covering Dean's belly.

"Oh, shit. Missed that." Dean rolled him, pulling off his shirt and bending to lick at the hollow of his throat.

"Yeah." Oh, yeah. Will petted, his other hand coming up to stroke the back of Dean's neck, his back, feeling the familiar scars under his hands as he moved, tilting his head back for more.

Dean was mapping his skin, moaning and licking and sucking, hands working at his waistband. His own hands found their way down under Dean's Levis, and he squeezed that double handful maybe too hard, but oh. Perfect.

Lips worried his nipple long enough for Dean to pop his fly and fish his cock out, holding him in a strong grip.

"Oh, Hell. Dean! God." That was the ticket. 'Course he wasn't gonna last five minutes, the man kept doing that.

"Yeah." Dean got his own jeans open and scooted up, pushing them together, hard and hot as August in that hand.

He just held on, pulling Dean hard against him, his own cock jerking, wet at the tip, hard as nails. "Missed this. Missed you."

"Yeah. Need you." Dean moaned against his lips, eyes hot. "Will..."

"Yeah." Pushing at Dean's jeans got them down where he could slide his fingers against Dean's hole, pressing carefully against it, humping that hand that held them together.

"Yeah..." Dean's hand was hard on his shoulder, the

good old boy rocking against him, tongue pushing in his mouth.

Hot and sweet, and more powerful than the rain outside their window. Will shouted into the kiss, body rocking as he came hard, just not able to hold it in. Dean tumbled along after him, that hand slick with his seed, the low moan desperate as Dean came.

They lay there panting for long moments, but sooner or later they'd get uncomfortable that way. Will nudged Dean with his shoulder. "Shower with me?"

Dean nodded, rolled off him and pulled them both off the bed. The bathroom shower curtain had been replaced and new tile put in since the last time he'd been home.

"Cowboy boots? Who sent us that?" He grinned, stripping out of his jeans, ogling Dean to beat the band.

"Aunt Nanette found it at the Wal-Mart." Dean chuckled. "It was too ugly not to keep."

"Hell, yes. Good thing, too. Makes me look pretty." That ass called to him again, and he rubbed it. "The showerhead, now, I'm thinking that was you."

Dean's skin flushed, heated, turned rosy just for him. "Might've been, yeah."

"I do like the way you think." His own skin was getting tight again, in some places anyway, and he figured they'd better get under the spray before he bent Dean over the sink and had at him.

The water was started, Dean managing to move around and never stop touching him. Never break contact. The room filled with steam right quick as it fought with the cold. "You ready to get in?"

"Yeah." Laughing at the pun that formed in his head, Will stepped into the shower, holding out a hand to Dean. And groaning. "Oh, fuck. That's nice."

Dean walked right into his arms and nodded. "Yeah. Oh, yeah."

Dean found the soap and started washing him, hands moving lazy as they stood together.

"Mmm." Not doing too well in the coherent department, was he? Dean didn't seem to mind, and they leaned on each other, hands moving on slick skin, warm and easy.

Dean settled, cheek on his shoulder, hands petting and massaging, mostly just holding on and being there.

Worked for him. The need had settled back into a dull ache, his pure exhaustion taking over, and it felt good just to let the water beat down on his back and hold Dean against him. Felt good just to be with the man again.

The touches lasted as long as the hot water did, Dean easing them both out before it got cold and ruined the relaxation.

They staggered back to bed, drying off as they went, and as much as Will wanted to prolong the homecoming, he was asleep as soon as his head hit the pillow. Because Dean was there, holding him, and it felt right. Damn, he missed the man when he was gone.

He woke up slow, the sound of Will's snoring so good, so right and he wasn't going to rush through it. The skin under his hand was warm, familiar.

Belonged right there in his bed.

The snoring cut off abruptly, Will starting half up in the bed before looking over at him. The sleepy grin he got was huge, stretched Will's face like to breaking. "Morning."

"Morning glory." Dean pulled Will over for a kiss, needing to taste that smile.

Will's smile turned evil, and he got a quick grope. "Sure is."

He laughed, feeling easy in his skin for the first time in days. Stupid, given he was home, but there it was, bald truth.

"Mmm." The touch went from joking to damned serious, Will stroking him, hand warm and firm. "Goddamn, you feel good, Dean."

"Nothing's like this, Will. Waking with you." He met Will's eyes, dead serious. "Glad you're home."

"You and me both." He got a kiss, long and sweet and almost chaste. "I was thinking..."

He swallowed down his immediate hoping. Will was young and he... wasn't. Will'd come home to stay one day, he knew it. Will knew it. He wasn't going to start pushing.

"Yeah, Ace?"

"Yeah. Well. I'm not setting the world on fire, you know? Ever since that last tumble I took, and tore up my shoulder and ribs." Will snuggled close, head on his chest. "And Gyspy, well, she's a doll, but with her stiff foreleg, she's not winning me any prizes."

He stroked that tore-up shoulder, nodding, heart beating hard. "You know you've got a place here, Will, a home. Or... if you want, we can look into trading one of the old tractors for another pony, a faster one."

A soft kiss dropped on his skin. "You're too damned good to me, cowboy. But, you know, it just doesn't hold the appeal it did, all that traveling. Not when I've got something to come home to. Getting to where I resent it, even. So. I guess I'm asking if I can come home to stay."

"No reason to ask for something that's always been yours." Oh, his chest hurt from wanting so hard. "I... I've been needing you, Will."

"Yeah. Been too damned hard, Dean. And I've been too stubborn." Will looked up at him, blue eyes so bright. "So, I'll stay."

"Yeah?" He nodded, watching those eyes. "Welcome home."

The smile widened until he thought it was going to slide right off Will's face. "Thank you."

He smiled back. Oh, God. He needed that. Needed to hear his Will was home to stay.

Dean leaned in and took a kiss. "Reckon the critters can wait twenty minutes for their feed?"

"Yeah." Will groped him again, that laugh light and happy. "I think they can manage."

"Good." He rolled Will over on top of him, his hands sliding down Will's upper thighs.

"Mmm." One leg slid to either side of his hips, and Will pressed down on him, rubbing. "You got anything slick, cowboy?"

"There might be a little something in the bedside table, yeah." Dean grinned, reaching over and digging under TV guides and a deck of cards and the latest Farmer's almanac to find the tube.

"Good. Want you in me, Dean." Will took the tube from him, and damned if Ace didn't slick up two fingers and reach behind, getting ready for him.

"Shit. Will, you're going make me shoot, just from watching." He reached out, stroking Will's prick, Will's belly.

"Not yet." Will gasped, arching against him, cock jumping in his hand. "Need. Need you, Dean."

"Yeah. Got me. You feel so hot. God, you're hot."

"You get me that way, Dean." Will grinned down at him, eyes wild, then squirted out more lube and reached for his cock, the cool gel almost a shock.

"Oh, damn..." He arched into the touch, hands squeezing Will's flesh. "Soon, Will. Soon."

"Yeah. Hell, yeah." Scooting up, Will put him into position, rising up to take him in, sliding down on him bit by bit.

"Oh..." Oh, God. It had been too damned long. Too long since he'd felt this heat, this pressure, this want.

A low moan came from deep in Will's body, he felt it vibrate through him, and Will started moving, hard and fast.

Dean reached out, hands wrapping around Will's hips, bringing them together.

"So empty..." Will pushed them hard, closing so tight on him.

"Fill you up, Will. Oh, God. Home. You're home." He bit his bottom lip, arching hard.

"Yeah. Love..." Will kissed him hard, leaning down, trapping Will's hot, wet cock between them. The kid kissed him hard, bruising him, probably to shut them both up. They were babbling.

Everything they needed to say was in the kiss anyway. In the kiss and the motion of their bodies and the slap of their skin.

Before long Will was losing the rhythm, body jerking on him, low moans coming from him as wet heat spread between them.

He grabbed Will's hip and pushed hard, riding out his wanting, his needing, spending himself with a quiet gasp, head pressed back hard into the pillows.

"Damn." Will flopped down on him, their sweat fusing them together.

"Uh-huh."

They rested for the rest of their twenty minutes. Will peeled away from him not long after, though, and grinned. "Well, cowboy. Guess it's time I started pulling my weight around here, huh?"

"I reckon." Dean grinned. "I cleaned out the chest of drawers for you last night, and half the closet."

"Oh." Something flashed in those blue eyes. Something

hot and real and good. “Then the least I can do is make you breakfast. Eggs and grits or pancakes and sausage?”

“Oh... pancakes.” He went and cleaned up before tugging on his briefs and jeans and an old flannel, him and Will moving around each other nice and easy. “I’m going to feed the critters and check on...”

He stopped shook his head. It was going to take a few days before checking on Miss Sadie wasn’t the first thing he did.

Will moved up behind him, arms going around his waist. “Check on Gypsy. She’ll be needing you. She’s plumb worn out.”

He nodded, patting Will’s hands. “Yeah. She needed to come home, live the good life.”

“She did. Just like the rest of us that you take care of.” A kiss landed on his neck, and he knew that was all Will had to say on the subject, knew that Ace felt the loss as keenly as he did. “Pancakes coming up. Don’t forget to use the feed I brought with me for Gypsy so she doesn’t swell up.”

“You put it in the barn or is it still in the truck?” He grabbed his hat on the way out the door, wincing at the cold wind. “Looks like fall’s here, sure enough.”

“In the barn. Unloaded before I came in. And it sure is.” Just as the door shut behind him he heard, “Damn, it’s good to be home.”

Yeah, yeah it was.

Epilogue

Dean whistled along with the radio, braiding long strips of leather. It was too damned cold to mend fence and too damned wet to ride and so he got his pack of spare leather out and started working it.

Made pretty decorations for the fancy saddles, too, and he felt good, sitting on the couch near the stove, coffee on the table.

If Will ever got in from doing his running? The world'd be just at perfect.

Like his wishing made it so, the door opened and Will came in, hands full of bags and boxes. "Damn. If I stayed out there anymore I'd turn into a duck."

He put the braid aside and got up to help with a grin, following Will into the kitchen. "D'you buy out Mineral Wells? What all'd you get?"

"Got that medicine we needed, and some flour and stuff we were getting low on. Oh, and I stopped by Mrs. Callahan's to fix that bad pipe she had? And she sent me home with fresh baked bread, apple crumb cake and gingerbread."

The gingerbread had to be why Will was grinning that way. He loved the stuff.

"Mm... Sounds good. How's Lucy's back? She staying

still like the doctor told her?" He helped unpack, putting stuff away, stealing nibbles of food as he went.

"Yeah. She's doing good. And that puppy we shipped over to old man Tabor? Growing like a weed and damned if the old fart doesn't look ten years younger." They got everything where it went and Will stole a piece of crumb cake out of his hand before kissing him hello.

Oh, and wasn't that nicer than any sweet known to man. Dean wrapped his arms around Will's waist, fingers stroking the small of Will's back as they kissed.

Will's arms came around his neck, lips warm and firm against his. "I'm gonna get you all wet."

"I'm not made of sugar, Ace. I'll manage." He deepened the kiss.

"Mmm." Will stopped arguing and started kissing like he meant it, curling his toes.

Damn, was there anything better on God's green Earth than this man, all warm and wanting and smelling of rain and ginger?

They pushed together nice and easy, until he was up against the kitchen counter, one of those long legs pushing between his.

"Mmm..." He let Will right on in, moaning his need into those lips. Christ, nothing set him off like this. Nothing made him needy as a teenaged boy in full bloom. Nothing but his Will.

"Yeah." Will chuckled, warm air puffing against his lips. "You make me hot as July, Dean."

"July where, though?" He winked, took another kiss, letting their laughter mix together.

That was the best part, that they could laugh together, even when they needed, even when that long thigh pressed against him and rubbed. He brushed his fingers through Will's hair, tongue playing with the stubble on thatupper lip, playing with the curve of that smile.

That made Will laugh again, made him rub their stubbly cheeks together. "I vote for the couch, cowboy. It's warm out there, and we can get a lot closer."

"I reckon you'd be warmer out of those wet clothes, too, Ace..." He started unbuttoning the little mother-of-pearl buttons, hunting skin.

"You know it." Will stepped back and let him work, shrugging out of the shirt when it was undone. Then Will went to work on his clothes. "Be even warmer with you out of yours. Body heat."

"Mmm... can't have you freezing, that's for damn sure." He leaned in, kissing and licking at Will's skin.

"No. That wouldn't do either of us a damned bit of good." Those lips moved down his neck, sharp teeth just nipping at him. "The couch, Dean."

"Uh-huh." He popped the top button of Will's jeans.

"Oh. Damn, that feels better." More nibbling, more chuckling, and Will got his jeans open too, pulling them together.

"This is not getting us... Oh, warm. Will. Not getting us to the couch."

"No. Let's dance, cowboy." It was awkward, with their jeans all but falling down, but Will got them dancing, shuffling out toward the living room, with its warm stove and couch.

They were laughing by the time they made it there, all wrapped up in each other, hands doing as much teasing as touching.

"Mmm. Better than gingerbread and fresh cream. Which I'm gonna have for dessert." Will got settled on the bottom, pulling him on top and squeezing his butt.

"Does that make me the main course?" He chuckled and took a kiss, rubbing their noses together.

"Every damned day." Will grinned up at him, making him feel like he'd hung the moon with those bright eyes loving on him like that.

"I'm a lucky man." He bent, brushing their lips together, tongue just peeking out to take a taste.

"Mmm." Sucking his tongue in, Will kissed him like there was no tomorrow.

Well now, that just pulled him all up into a big old knot. He moaned into Will's mouth, toes curling. Those strong hands moved over his butt and his back, massaging as they kissed. Sweet and hot and more like dessert than the main course, their kisses making him tingle.

"Damn, Ace. You're something else." He slid his hand down Will's belly, petting with a long, slow stroke.

"Yeah? I think you're the special one, cowboy. But we won't waste time arguing." They kissed some more, long and sweet and deep.

He let his hands pet and rub and explore, searching out each little soft place, the ticklish spots, the sweet spots that made his cowboy cry out and shiver. He got the same treatment from Will, those sweet hands sliding over his scars then dipping beneath his lowered jeans to tease his balls. Oh, Christ on a crutch, that felt better than a cool breeze in August. He moaned, mouth sliding down to taste the salt and rain and sweet of Will's throat.

"God, you feel good in my hands, cowboy." Petting him, cradling him, Will nibbled and licked along his neck and chest.

Being right at home was always good. He moaned as Will's lips found a little hot spot and he shivered, goosebumps coming right up.

They just stayed right there, lazily tasting and kissing and loving all over, Will moaning under him, spreading wider to let them rub together, hot and slick.

He managed to get a hand wrapped around their pricks, squeezing them both together nice and tight. It felt good -- hell, better than good. It made him tight in his belly, made him take a hard kiss.

Will opened right up to his kiss, the hottest little noises coming from him. Long fingers teased him, going from his balls to his hole, pushing lightly. Oh, that just set him off like a punk to a fuse and he arched, hips moving just that much harder, that much faster.

"Dean. God, love. That's... oh." Will pumped up into his hand, rubbing against him like crazy. One finger found its way inside him, sliding rough, making serious friction.

"Oh, yeah. Will... Gonna make me... Oh..." He found Will's rhythm then, fast and hard and just sweet, raw wanting and lost his words quicker than a televangelist facing St. Peter, just went all feeling.

Will grunted, moving under him like the bucking horse of the year, crying out against his lips as heat splashed over his hand.

That was all it took, come shooting right from him as his balls ached, leaving him gasping and shaking like a newborn colt.

"Damn."

"Yeah. Hell of a meal, Dean." Will laughed, shaking them both.

A wild hair got him and he raised his slick hand to his lips licking it clean, feeling Will's eyes on him. "Mm... yessir."

"Oh..." Will just stared at him, eyes stunned and loving. "Damn."

Oh, but Will made him feel like the sexiest thing walking and he was trembling when he leaned down to lick Will's lips. "Yeah."

"Mmm." Will took the kiss, moving against him like they hadn't just come all over each other. "Better than gingerbread and cream."

"Better than anything, Ace." He grinned, happy and

hot all through. "Thank the good Lord we can have it all."